T0147037

Wings in a Jar

Wings in a Jar

Albert Rodriguez

WINGS IN A JAR

*This is a work of fiction. All of the characters, names, incidents,
organizations, and dialogue in this novel are either the products
of the author's imagination or are used fictitiously.*

iUniverse books may be ordered through booksellers or by contacting:

iUniverse
1663 Liberty Drive
Bloomington, IN 47403
www.iuniverse.com
1-800-Authors (1-800-288-4677)

*Because of the dynamic nature of the Internet, any web addresses or links contained in
this book may have changed since publication and may no longer be valid. The views
expressed in this work are solely those of the author and do not necessarily reflect the
views of the publisher, and the publisher hereby disclaims any responsibility for them.*

*Any people depicted in stock imagery provided by Getty Images are models,
and such images are being used for illustrative purposes only.
Certain stock imagery © Getty Images.*

ISBN: 978-1-5320-7225-3 (sc)
ISBN: 978-1-5320-7555-1 (hc)
ISBN: 978-1-5320-7224-6 (e)

Library of Congress Control Number: 2019903665

Print information available on the last page.

iUniverse rev. date: 05/17/2019

With love to
my mom, Delia;
my sister, Rosanne; and
my best friend, Michael C. Ryan—
and in loving memory of my brother, Raul Jr.

CONTENTS

CHAPTER 1

Beginning Cycles

Most of the time I would walk alone to school slowly. I lived in a suburban neighborhood in Los Angeles County, mainly made up of old homes built around the 1920s and some apartments. Most of the houses had open lawns, without fences to protect them from the outside world. The houses and apartments that were gated or fenced in were private and mysterious. My eyes were always moving: to the left, to the right, down the street. Every tenth step, I would turn around to check behind me too. I needed to be on alert for any kids who could make me feel uncomfortable. I hate to admit it, but what made me so afraid was the emotional beast of shyness that lived inside me. I would become so stiff that my shoulders would ache by the time I got to school every morning. Then, as I came close to the place where the Alves family lived, my heart would beat hard, and my ears would become hot. I did not want the kids who lived behind the house by the sidewalk to come out and say something to me. Then it actually happened one morning as I walked to school.

Javier and his two brothers came out quickly from behind the house, and Javier said, "Hey, Quattuor, what's up?"

I looked down and turned slightly in his direction and whispered, "Hi." Then I walked quickly away from him and his brothers toward school.

Once the bell rang and I was seated in class, I felt a little more at ease. I liked my first grade teacher, Miss Cot, except for the way she smelled. She wore a strong, stinky perfume. Reading comprehension and cursive writing were my favorite subjects. There were these Sullivan books that ranged from the most basic to the most advanced level. Every book was a different color, which made it exciting. Orange was the most basic, and green was a thicker, more advanced book. On the right side of the pages were the answers that you would cover up with a white cardboard marker. After you read the sentences, you would fill in the blanks on an answer sheet and then take away the card to check your answers. When you finished the book, you would take a test that the teacher corrected. If you passed, you would go on to the next book. It was fun but hard work to finish these little books.

What made the book program more exciting was this girl, Elena, who sat next to me. She was different from the other girls because her thick black hair was very long, and the front part of it would hang down on the side to cover one eye. We were the most advanced students in the Sullivan series program, so we would compete with each other to see who could get to the next book first. Then she started cheating by skipping pages and would take the test right away. Most of the time she passed the tests. She was smart and sneaky.

I remember one time I left my seat to go to the restroom, and when I came back, I found my book on a different page and couldn't remember where I was in the book. I flipped back two pages. *That's not it. I already did that*, I thought. I flipped forward ten pages. *Not there either.* I snuck a glance at Elena. She was studiously moving along quickly through the pages of a new book. A lot of time was wasted before I could find the correct page. I didn't dare try to skip pages. I had much respect for the Sullivan program. I suspected that Elena was the one who'd changed the page of my book. I was angry and didn't want to ever talk to her again.

After the weekend, on Monday, Elena and I became closer. She asked me if I'd like to walk her home after school. I replied, "Only if you stop changing the pages in my book."

She agreed to try her best not to do it and said she was just playing. We walked in the same direction that I normally walked home every day. When we got to the third block, however, she guided me toward the left away from the park that I walked through to get home. I started to worry a little because I didn't tell my mom that I was going to walk anyone home, and I knew she would worry if I didn't show up at my regular time. I asked Elena how many blocks it was to her house from where we were standing. "Only eight blocks," she said.

Since I'd agreed to walk her home beforehand, we proceeded on the journey toward her house. I made her aware of how the sidewalk was divided into little squares. I told her that we had to step into each square without touching the lines and count each one so we could learn how many squares there were to her home. She liked the idea and said she had done this before but did not remember how many squares it was to her place. After about twenty-six squares, she asked me something, and we lost track and had to start the count again. Before long we reached a smooth sidewalk without any more squares. I did happen to keep track of the blocks, however, and after the sixth block, I asked, "Are we almost there?"

"Yes, it's not too much farther," she replied happily.

My hands started to sweat because it was getting late and I thought I would have been home by then. It wasn't until after the eighth block that I became angry and started to breathe through my mouth because we were still walking. "I thought you said you lived eight blocks away."

"Just a couple more blocks. We're almost there," she said nicely.

After eleven blocks, we finally reached her house behind a black steel gate. It looked private and scary with its steel-barred windows and closed shades and curtains. As Elena unlocked the front gate, all I wanted to do was turn around and run home. Her mom and dad opened the front door as we headed up the steep concrete steps and were kind and receptive. They asked me if I wanted to stay for dinner. I told them "no thanks" because I had to get home. My mom was probably worried, therefore they called my mom for me, and yes, she was worried but said it was okay if I stayed for dinner. However, I felt nervous. The sun was starting to go down. It was becoming so late.

"I have a lot of homework to do and have a stomachache. I'll come over next time," I said in a worried voice.

"Okay, next time then," said Elena's mother. "I'll call your mom and let her know you're on the way."

"Bye, son. Rain check on the dinner," said the dad. "Elena, open the gate for him."

At the gate, Elena said, "Bye. I'll see you at school tomorrow."

"Bye," I said and quickly started down the sidewalk. When I turned the corner, I ran the rest of the way home.

CHAPTER 2

First Fight at School

After the second grade, my focus changes from the classroom to nutrition and lunch in the schoolyard. Handball is my favorite game to play during nutrition and lunch. Everything in my life feels so controlled except when I'm playing handball with someone against the faded pink board. Although I like the timed schedules and structure that school life provides—go to this class here, go to that class there; go to nutrition now, go to lunch after math class in room 8—when I play handball, I am in control of my own destiny. I can hit the ball as hard as I want and make split decisions on hitting the ball into a sharp, low bounce off the board to cause my opponent to miss the ball. If you do not hit the ball back, you lose the game and have to sit down on the bench at the end of the line and wait for your turn to come up again. I am one of the top five players, which is pretty good for a third grader. Today, however, the order is disrupted at handball time, which I play during the fifteen-minute nutrition break. I run toward the handball bench and wind up fifth in line.

I stand up for a second to pull up my pants, and suddenly, Douglas appears in front of me on the bench. Others have cut in line before, and it bothers me, but they've never cut directly in front of me.

"No cutting," I say to Douglas.

"Hey, man, I was here," he claims.

"No way. Go to the back of the line. No cutting," I say.

"I was here. I don't know what you're talking about," he says.

I look around the yard and don't see the yard lady. I get up and attempt to squeeze in and sit down between student number four and him; however, he squeezes against the student tightly, leaving me no room to sit between them. This leaves me no choice but to look for the yard lady. I head toward the space between two buildings that separate the kindergarten building from the first-through-sixth-grade building. I don't see the yard lady, so I head back toward the handball area and turn to look into the fenced kindergarten area. There are a few little kids in the sandbox. It is a small paddock-like area without the hay and horses. It used to seem like such a fun, large play area that I could escape to when I was in kindergarten. How odd. As I turn away and peer toward the handball court, I see Douglas receive the handball. He is up to start the game. I run over as fast I can and shout to him, "It's my turn, not yours, you cutter," and I yank the big dull-pink ball from his hands.

His chest puffs out, and he gets real close to me and says, "Give me the ball!"

"No, it's my turn," I respond. "You cut in line."

"Just let him go. It's not worth it," says one of the girls on the bench.

Douglas pushes me hard, and I push him back just as hard.

"Here, you can have my place in line next," says the girl at the front of the bench.

Suddenly his fist comes toward my jaw, and I block it with my left arm. His left fist quickly follows though, and he hits me in the lower jaw. We break out into a fistful of blows for what seems like a long time, but it must have been only about ten seconds.

"Break it up!" hollers the yard lady. She blows her whistle. "Break it up!" she yells again as some other male students help her separate us.

The bell rings, and surprisingly, the yard lady tells us to go to class. I thought we were going to be taken to the office and that I would be in a lot of trouble. She must have known that the two of us were never a problem until this day. And I don't believe either of us got hurt too bad.

Once I go to class, I can't concentrate on the vocabulary assignment because I'm thinking about the fight. I realize that I fought back because Douglas pushed me first. This is my personal rule. I will never fight anyone unless they touch me first. And if they touch me, I will fight back no matter what.

CHAPTER 3

Frozen

After third grade some problems ensue with some bullying students. Out in the yard during nutrition, a swarm of ten thugs surround me on my way to sit on one of the lunch benches. These are the older sixth grade boys who always hang out in groups. "Hey, you dorky-ass nerd, why you so quiet?" asks this short, three-and-a-half-foot, tough-looking guy.

The others stare me down with their chests puffed out as they lean toward me just inches from my face. I can't respond. I am frozen. "Say something!" says the supershort guy. "I'm gonna kick your ass so bad if you don't talk."

The group moves in closer, and a bulky guy threatens, "We're gonna kick your ass so bad, and you're gonna cry for yo mama."

"Let me go," I say and make my lowered hands into fists.

"What's going on here?" asks the yard lady as she approaches the hovering crowd with me in the middle.

"Nothing," one guy says.

"Nada, everything's cool," says another as the group breaks away in different directions.

I stand there rigid, and the yard lady asks me, "Everything okay? Were those guys bothering you?"

"No," I reply. "They were just asking me some questions about my cousin."

The yard lady nods in response, and I quickly walk away to the steps of the main building with my legs feeling like rubber bands. Students are not allowed to be on the steps, so I wait at the foot of the steps and hold the rail with one hand. I want the bell to ring so I can go into the building and my class as quickly as possible. I'm going to tell my mom later to switch me to another school because bullies torture me a lot during nutrition and lunch, now that I think of it.

Other bullies my age try to take my lunch away from me when I sit on the benches outside under the covered eating area. Their names are Alejandro and Rogelio. They take anyone's lunch they can but seem to pick on me the most. They tell me to give them my hamburger or fries, for example, and when I say no, they threaten to kick my ass later. Sometimes I give them part of my lunch because others are watching and I don't want attention from other students. However, my rule still applies: if they touch me physically, I will fight. For instance, Javier tried to take my whole lunch tray once, and I pulled it back from his grasping hands.

He said, "Give it to me!"

I said, "No!" loudly and stood stiff and ready to fight.

He backed away and said, "Dude, keep your lunch, lil' sissy!"

CHAPTER 4

Spelling and Fifth Grade

A year has passed, and all the former sixth grade thugs have moved on to junior high. The feeling of sadness and fear has disappeared when I go out to the yard for nutrition and lunch. Those bad boys owned the school, but there are other bullies who continue to harass me. Sometimes I feel like I don't want to live anymore, but I must continue. I need to finish what I set out to do, which is graduate from the sixth grade.

What's exciting about fifth grade is that I learned that I excel at spelling. I just spent a wonderful Sunday evening at a Dodger game with Ms. Tamiko, my English teacher, and her family for winning the spelling bee in her class. It was a lot of fun. Ms. Tamiko, her husband, nephew, and niece joined us. She is my favorite teacher in fifth grade. I feel comfortable around her family too. They are nice people who seem to like me.

Mr. Baun, on the other hand, is not so cool. I feel uncomfortable around him because he is serious and businesslike. He makes us write our name, date, period, and class on our papers in the upper right-hand corner and a title in the center. If we don't do it correctly, he gives us back our work with no credit. He also makes us staple our work with the staple vertically placed. One time during nutrition, a girl gave me a piece of gum right when the bell rang. As I walked up the steps in the building, Mr. Baun was walking down the steps on the other side of the rail.

"Are you chewing gum?" he asked loudly in a serious voice as he looked at me with stone-cold eyes.

I nervously swallowed the gum and said, "No."

He turned his hand with the palm facing up and pointed two fingers at me and curled them in to show that he wanted me to follow him. When we got to the bottom of the stairs and into the hallway, he said, "You're going to pick up one wastebasket full of trash during nutrition tomorrow for chewing gum and another wastebasket full of trash for lying."

At lunch I picked up the trash and felt like everyone was watching me. I started to count the pieces of trash I picked up. When I got to ten, I started to count all over again. After I finished, I told the yard lady what Mr. Baun wanted me to do and if I could take the wastebasket up to him to show him. She said, "No, sweetie, just dump it in the big green dumpster, and I'll let him know."

Today, however, is an exciting time in Mr. Baun's class because we are doing a spelling bee. The very first word is *abolitionist*, and most of the kids cannot spell it. There are only four of us left standing, me included, who can spell the word. The next word is *abolitionism*. Two of the students cannot spell it so they are out. It's just me and Jennie now. The next word is *bicycle*. Jennie is first up. "B-y-c-I … no, b-i-c-i-c-l-e," she spells.

"Is this your final attempt?" asks Mr. Baun.

"Yes," says Jennie.

"That is incorrect," says Mr. Baun.

"Quattuor, spell the word *bicycle*."

"B-y-c … no wait, b-i-c-y-c-l-e," I say nervously.

"Is that your final response?" asks Mr. Baun.

"Yes," I say. My face feels hot.

"That is correct. Quattuor, as the winner of the spelling bee, you have won a free lunch tomorrow at the park with me, Mr. Haley, and three other students who also won the spelling bee from the other classes."

At home that night, I toss and turn and can't sleep. I'm nervous about going to lunch with Mr. Baun. It seems more like a punishment than a reward. I don't want to go. Maybe I'll tell my mom I'm sick in the morning so I don't have to go to school. Nah, I decide against it. Mr. Baun will see right through me and probably *fail* me. And every time I look at him, I will not be able to face him. Let me try something else. I am too freaked out.

"One thousand ten, one thousand nine, one thousand eight …" I whisper from bed, lying on my back, I count all the way down to 1,001.

I figure this will make me sleepy. It doesn't work so I start to count again, but this time from nine. "One thousand nine, one thousand eight, one thousand seven," and so on until I reach 1,001.

It still doesn't work; therefore, I start the count again with 1,008 and so on until I reach 1,001. I continue with this order until somewhere around 1,004 I finally fall asleep.

"Get up now and get dressed!" yells my mom the next morning.

I feel so sleepy but go to school even though I don't want to. It seems dreamlike putting so much worry toward the lunch with Mr. Baun. However, when it comes time for lunch, I walk slowly and nervously to his classroom. Mr. Haley, the special ed teacher, is there and only one other student. We go to Mr. Baun's long gray car, and he drives us to Papa Don's to get a sandwich and then over to the park. Under the shady trees, the student and I sit on one bench while Mr. Baun and Mr. Haley sit four benches away from us. The kid from Mr. Haley's class is not easy to talk to. I sit across the table from him and have to ask him questions in order for him to speak.

"What is your name? I ask.

"Kyle," he says loudly.

He doesn't say anything after that so after a few minutes I ask, "Did you win the spelling bee too?"

"Yes," he says.

"Have you ever been to this park before?" I ask a minute later.

He doesn't answer. Instead he claps his hands loudly in the air to kill flying insects and pounds the palm of his hand on the table hard to kill insects that he feels need to die. It makes me uncomfortable, and I start to get mad. After a few minutes pass, the cool air on my face makes me calm down. I think about the bullies who have bothered me and hated me. Kyle is not like this. I shouldn't be mad at him just because he kills flying insects and doesn't speak unless I ask him a question.

Suddenly he laughs out loud and asks, "Do you want my pickle?" as he removes it from the sandwich wrapping.

I think, *No way, 'cause you touched it with your insect-killing hands.* But I say, "Yeah sure," because I think I might hurt his feelings if I say no.

He hands it to me, and I put it on the side of my sandwich wrapping.

"You want to go look at the river?" he asks.

"Yeah sure," I say. *This guy is not so bad after all*, I think.

CHAPTER 5

A Force to Be Reckoned With

A month passes by before Mr. Baun gives another spelling bee. This time there are new rules about who can be in the spelling bee. When he announces, "You can only be a part of the spelling bee if you're getting a C or better in the class," I attempt to make eye contact with him, but he does not look my way.

I clearly see why he did this. He doesn't like me. He regrets taking a quiet student to lunch who does not speak to him unless he asks a question. I'm sure I annoy him. He wants a talkative and interesting student to win the spelling bee.

Why do I have a D in his class? First of all he is too strict. Every class assignment has to be finished during class. In addition, we have homework. This doesn't work for me; I never finish my class assignments during class because I strive for perfection. My cursive writing has to be perfect, and my answers have to be correct to the best of my ability. If my writing is not perfect, I feel bad and have to start all over again. I know he doesn't grade on neat writing, and

I'm not sure if he grades on correct answers. I only know for sure that he wants assignments completed on time. Sometimes I cannot finish my homework because he gives too much, and half the time I don't understand it.

During class, Mr. Baun, the meanest and most serious history teacher, keeps me paying attention in class because I don't want him to call on me and not be able to answer his questions. Every time he calls on me and I cannot answer his questions, I become embarrassed. For instance, he asked me recently, "Where did Japan launch a surprise attack on the US, December 7, 1941?"

I shrug my shoulders and say quietly, "I'm not sure."

"Obviously you didn't study last night!" he remarks.

I feel bad after that because, although Mr. Baun is a strict and cold-hearted teacher, I want to please him. I don't want to be a bad student. I think I can do better. I will stay up all night if I have too so I can finally finish all of my homework.

CHAPTER 6

My Cousin and Me at Twelve

It isn't until I turn twelve that I see life in a different way. I am a latchkey kid. My mom works and goes to school; however, my aunt lives next door and keeps an eye out for my brother, my sister, and me. No one is home so I head over to my aunt's house to talk to my cousin Abby, short for Abhaya. The name comes from her dad's side; he is part Hawaiian and Japanese. Her mother and my mother are sisters, who are mainly of Mexican and Spanish descent. Abby and I are the same age. She is always crazy happy about something. I don't know anyone more full of life than she is. Immediately she grabs my hand and pulls me into her room. When the two of us are together, we cause trouble. Right away she starts to tell me about her friends and about a guy who likes her. Then she brings up Javier. "Remember the Alves? Little Javier is in one of my classes. He remembers you. He said you would always ignore him when he'd say hi to you."

Surprised, I say, "I would say hi to him."

"All I know is he said, 'Your cousin is ass-weird!'" says Abby, and she giggles loudly.

Suddenly my ears begin to feel hot, and my shoulders tighten. It is the same feeling I'd get when I walked to Tarnanza Elementary School in the morning. "He doesn't like me. A lot of those guys at school didn't like me. They were always picking on me," I say and pout. "Remember when I used to tell you about the times all those guys would bother me and you would go and tell them to leave me alone?"

With a gleam in her eye, Abby moves her head to one side and says, "Remember Rogelio? I told him, 'Leave my cousin alone. 'You're gonna have to go through me first if you touch him.'"

"Yeah, he never bothered me again after that. He liked me after that and protected me from other enemies."

"Oh, how you made me fight your battles." She exhales.

"I never told you to protect me. I said never to tell anyone, and you wouldn't listen. You would tell all those guys everything," I say defensively. "I've been picked on by so many kids and even teachers, and you had nothing to do with it. You just go to school every day with all your friends and have a great time and shampoo your hair with mayonnaise so it can be shiny while I live a life of hell every day."

CHAPTER 7

A Shortcut through the Old Haunted Mansion

When it comes to outdoor activities like going to the public pool or the river, playing sports, or jogging, I hang out with my brother, cousin Hiro, and their friends. On our way to the Brookside Pool by the Rose Bowl, I tell my brother, his friend Devin, and my cousin Hiro about an idea for a shortcut. "Let's cut through the Old Haunted Mansion," I suggest. "This is the tenth block away from where we live and a good way to take a shortcut."

It's not really a mansion, but it is one of the bigger homes in our neighborhood. The right and left sides have round towers, and its windows are in the shape of arrow loops like a castle. It would have been better to call it the Old Haunted Castle, but as long as I can remember, it has been known as the Old Haunted Mansion through the grapevine of kid gossip in the neighborhood. The reason it is thought to be haunted is because the legend goes that a father murdered his young fifteen-year-old daughter in her bedroom in one of the towers when he found out she was pregnant. They say if you walk there at night during a full moon, you can hear her screaming and that some have seen the ghost of a young girl in a white gown appear at an arrow-loop window in one of the round towers. I don't believe any of this. I think kids just like to make up stories.

We get to the front of the house easily enough because it is not gated or fenced in. We creep quietly onto the driveway that curves around by the front door. We look up at the front of the house. There are no visible signs of movement at the windows, so we proceed cautiously to the side of the house. It is a long, narrow passageway to the back of the house. As I suspected, the hillside slopes down farther than the eye can see with overgrown ivy, prickly bushes, trees, tall unkept grass, and weeds.

"You guys up for it?" I ask the group.

"Hell yeah," says my brother with a wide-eyed stare.

"What if there's a gate at the bottom that we can't get through?" asks Devin.

"We'll just climb back up," I say.

"Screw it; it's worth a try," says Hiro, the youngest one of us.

As we head down, it is even more treacherous than it looks. Some of these bushes have sharp thorns on the leaves, and my pants, socks, and shoes become covered with what us kids call "stickies." Their proper name is spikelets, the flowering part of the grass.

My cousin Hiro slips on something slimy and lands on his behind before he slides about five feet down the slope. A big tree branch stops him from sliding down any farther. We all laugh out loud. RJ, my brother, who is farther down the slope than the rest of us, climbs up to reach Hiro first. "You all right, man?" he asks as he pulls him up with one hand.

Hiro starts to laugh. "Let's get the hell out of here. Whose idea was this?" he asks. He turns around to look at me coming down the slope with Devin by my side.

"It's not my fault that you fell. You were going too fast," I say half-jokingly.

Now that Hiro is standing up, he realizes that the back of his pants and part of his shirt are covered in green slime and mud. "Oh man, my mom's gonna kill me," he announces.

"Just tell her that we took a shortcut by the river and you fell in," suggests RJ.

"No, she's not gonna believe that. You know my mom," says Hiro.

"Okay, here's the plan," I say. "RJ, since you're the fastest, run down to the bottom and see if there's a way out for sure. If not, we can climb back up before somebody else slips. And, Hiro, when we get to the river, wash your pants and shirt in the current."

We all agree to the plan, and RJ quickly reaches the bottom before the rest of us. "Hey, you guys!" shouts RJ from somewhere below. "Turn around; there's a fence."

"We can climb it," I yell back.

"No, there's a dog on the other side," he yells.

We continue to walk down a little farther not wanting to believe him because we've come so far. Then there he is. I can see him standing by a chain-link fence with two German shepherds on the other side barking viciously at him.

"Okay, let's go back up," I say with irritation.

Climbing up the hill is much more difficult than climbing down. Every five feet takes about five minutes.

"Hey, guys, where did that come from?" says Devin, pointing at a huge jagged rock peering out of the slope. "That wasn't there before," he adds as we look at its immense size.

"I don't know, dude," says my brother to his friend. "Let's just go that way to the side and climb up," he suggests as he points to the right.

We follow RJ, who makes his way up carefully to the right. The sun starts to bake the top of my head. And just when I think we're making our way back quickly, a huge fallen tree blocks our path.

"Guys, we're going the wrong way. I don't think we came down this way," says Devin.

"Yeah, you're right. I think we came down way more toward the left," I reply. "Let's just keep going to the right and go around it."

As we make our way toward the right, the top end of the fallen tree becomes small enough to climb over.

"Guys, I gotta rest," says Hiro with a flushed tomato-red face.

"Dude, just get over the trunk at least," says RJ.

RJ and I reach out a hand and pull Hiro up over the fallen tree.

"Guys, I gotta rest," repeats Hiro with labored breathing.

"It's hot. You can rest when we get out of this hellhole," I shout.

I turn around and continue to climb the thorny slope. Devin follows right behind me. RJ, not wanting to leave his favorite cousin behind, decides to push him up the hill from behind. We reach the top, and I put my index finger to my lips and quietly blow out, "Shhh," before we proceed down the narrow side of the old mansion.

As we come out toward the front, Hiro says out loud, "Phew! I'm thirsty. I need some water."

"Dude, shut the hell up," commands RJ loudly.

"You guys," I whisper through gritted teeth.

I hear a sound like something unlatching followed by a low rumbling noise. We all look up toward the front of the house and see a bald-headed man stick his head out the window and shout, "Hey, this is private property!"

"Sorry, we were looking for someone ..." I start to say.

"You're trespassing on private property," snaps the bald man. "Helen, get the gun!"

The back of my neck and head start to tingle before all of us take off running as fast as we can down the block toward home. None of us stop until we reach the front yard where me and my brother live. My legs are shaking and feel like they're made out of springy rubber bands. Everyone is panting for breath, and Hiro is on his back gasping for air.

"Come on," I say. "Let's get inside. What if he comes in his car looking for us?"

We all head toward the porch, and I nervously drop the keys before I can get them into the lock of my front door. As soon as we get inside, Hiro says, "I need water."

I give Hiro some water as soon as we get in. How different he is than his older sister, Abby. Hiro is a nice younger cousin. My brother and I pick on him a lot. We shouldn't, but it's fun. I remember this Marine guy across the street called Hiro handicapped just because he wasn't as good at sports as my brother and me. For one, he would flip his wrist to pitch a baseball. It was because he is double-jointed. This marine guy was not legit though: he picked on him because he was AWOL. What I mean by that is he escaped from the military while he was still in training. He could not handle it.

Hiro's mother, my aunt, is handicapped. One leg is shorter than the other due to polio; therefore, this disturbed her a lot. Abby, on the other hand, is confident and a control kind of girl. If she doesn't like what you suggest, she will toss you aside. What I realize is when I'm with Abby, I'm much bolder and willing to cause havoc if needed. With Hiro, however, I'm more protective of him, everyone, and surrounding situations. He makes me feel different in a way that I don't have to be something other than who I am, I think.

CHAPTER 8

Fight Season

Fight season happens every year. It occurs every spring at Tarnanza Elementary School. Many kids start to fight for some reason, but I don't know why. I wonder if this will continue when I move on to junior high in the fall. Elena and Rogelio are going to fight today after school in the park. Everyone knows about it. Even the principal, I'm sure. The bell rings for lunch, and I drag myself out of math class. I hate being out in the yard. I quickly make it to the lunch line and then sit kind of close to other students once I get my food inside the cafeteria. I ask first if anyone is sitting where I want to sit, and one girl shakes her head, but the others ignore me. I sit with a personal-space distance from everyone to let them know that I'm aware we are not friends—I just need somewhere to sit. I keep my head down as the others lower their voices to a loud whisper. There are three boys and two girls. I look up slightly and see one guy with his arm around one of the girls, and the group starts to laugh about something someone said in their private conversation.

I feel so uncomfortably alone. I feel like I'm disturbing their private lunchtime so I get up, throw the rest of my lunch in the trash, and quickly walk away. I don't like myself. Why do I have to be so shy, tall, skinny, and dark?

"Hey, Quattuor, where ya going?" asks Sheila. She is seated with a group of four girls at a table by the cafeteria door that exits into the hall.

"Outside. I ate lunch already."

"Hi, Quattuor," says Elena. "Hardly see you anymore since they switched my English class."

"Yeah, it's been boring without you."

"Is my sister doing all her work?" asks Elena.

"Yeah, she even finishes early sometimes. I'll see you all later. Bye," I state nervously as I make my exit.

I go into the yard and sit down on the elongated bench at the handball court. Two girls hit the large pink ball back and forth for a long time until a guy at the front of the line says, "Okay, that was over thirty hits."

The rules changed after fourth grade because some of the girls would hit the ball back and forth lightly so they wouldn't mess up, and they would continue to play for long periods of time so no one else would get a turn.

As I sit on the bench and realize that I may never get my turn, from the corner of my eye I notice many students start to move in one direction. Some students start to run. I jump up from the bench and ask nearby students what's going on. "A fight," someone shouts as he leaps over the edge of the skinny bench.

I leave the bench and look toward the buildings and see a swarm of students tightly packed together. As I slowly make my way to the crowd, others continue to run and add themselves to the growing mass. The yard lady's whistle blows from inside the swarm, and additional adult staff, which includes administrators and other teachers, come shouting in loud, authoritative voices, "Break it up, break it up. Stop … get back!"

Some of the students on the outskirts back up slightly and move to one side to let the adults into the penetrating crowd. After about twenty seconds, the crowd breaks open to one side with two adults holding onto Rogelio. They move him swiftly toward the main building. Another adult holds onto Elena, with the yard lady in back, leading her to the office as well. It's hard to believe these two got in a fight. Rogelio always teased Elena, but she would ignore him. If he persisted, sometimes she would say, "Go away." Other times she would just give him a half smile before walking away.

Elena continues to be a unique girl with special qualities. I never thought about it before; I've always taken her friendship for granted. She has always treated me with the greatest kindness since that one time we walked to her house in second grade. She's a great listener because she listens to every word I have to say, and she never rambles on about herself when I tell her a story. I think she might like me because she gets really close to me when I talk to her sometimes. I've never noticed this before because I don't have feelings for her that way. She's a tomboy, not my type. Besides, we hardly have seen each other since second grade because we never had a class together after that. From now on I'm going to be supernice to her, and I hope that she didn't get into too much trouble.

My life seems to break up somehow. Sometimes I go through certain events, and other times I am a completely different person. I hope there is nothing wrong with me. It's like I'm divided into four different selves. I act a certain way when I go to church, but I'm different at home, different with cousins, and different at school.

CHAPTER 9

The Cat Incident

It is now summer break after my graduation from sixth grade. The huge burden of elementary school life has been lifted away. I excitedly make my way over to see my cousin Abby.

"Let's go see if Jenna's home," says Abby enthusiastically.

I agree, and she goes to ask her mom for permission. Jenna's house is just down the block on the corner. A black, orange, and white cat runs along the sidewalk by Jenna's chain-link fence. Ruddy, Jenna's big dog, starts to bark repeatedly at the cat.

"I hate that cat," mutters Abby. "It tried to hurt Pepper."

Pepper is my cousin's cat. "Oh, maybe it was just lonely," I respond in a sympathetic manner.

"I hate all cats except Pepper. Look at how that derelict cat teases Ruddy. There's a way to poison cats."

"Really?" My curiosity peaks.

"Put aspirin in their milk. That'll kill them," Abby states with a cold look in her eyes.

"I don't think any cat deserves to die. They don't really wanna bother anybody," I state defensively.

"Jenna … Jenna!" shouts Abby toward the back porch steps from outside the chain-link fence.

After about forty seconds, Jenna comes down the steps toward the gate. "Hey, guys," greets Jenna with the biggest smile a person can have. Her smile is always so big that you can see her gums, braces, and big teeth all at once. She has a huge amount of compassion for everyone and everything. She quickly unlocks the gate, opens it ever so slightly, and squeezes through the narrow space before quickly locking it back up.

"What do you guys wanna do today?" asks Jenna.

"Let's go to the record store," answers Abby.

We all agree that it is a great idea, and Abby and I go to get permission from our moms. "No," says my mom when I call her at work. "You need to get dinner started at four o'clock."

I tell my cousin and Jenna the bad news. Abby also cannot go because my aunt has an appointment, and Abby has to stay home and keep an eye on Hiro—her little brother, my cousin—and clean her bedroom. Once my aunt leaves, Abby becomes furious and picks up clothes from the bed and the bedroom floor and throws them toward the open closet. She pounds her fists on the mattress and screams. Jenna's mouth frowns into an oval before she calmly says, "I better go. Call me later, okay? We'll go another time."

After Jenna leaves, I say to Abby, "You know how you said that you hate cats? I have an idea. Let's collect twenty cats from around the neighborhood and put them in your house. When your mom comes home and opens the door, there'll be cats running everywhere … meow!"

Abby laughs out loud and says, "Okay, let's do it!"

We walk together with Hiro on our expedition. It isn't too difficult to find cats in the neighborhood. We capture each cat one by one and put them in my aunt's house. The ones that are too squirrelly in our arms we let go. We travel within a circumference of ten blocks to find all twenty cats. After cat number twenty is put into the house, we peer into the darkness from outside the screen door. It is quiet. We hear no meowing, noise, or movement at all. When my aunt comes home, we appear more at ease and pick berries from the hedge alongside the front porch. My aunt goes inside, and within about thirty seconds, she yells, "Abby and Hiro, what are all these cats doing in here?"

The three of us burst out with suppressed laughter and quickly run into the house. A large cat darts across the living room into the kitchen. "The screen door was open when I came out of my room," explains Abby.

Another cat runs out from the corner, crashes into the wall, turns around, and heads toward us. We scream, and Hiro grabs hold of me around the waist. Two more cats come out of nowhere and run into the hallway toward the bedrooms. "Open the screen door," yells my aunt.

Abby leaps to open it, and a cat immediately jumps out toward freedom. Meanwhile my aunt moves into the kitchen, retrieves the broom, and says, "Shoo!" as she swats the broom at some tricky cats hiding in the kitchen. "The three of you get in here and get these cats out of here!" shouts my aunt.

A cat jumps toward Abby, Hiro, and me, and we run outside. Hiro keeps on running down the block, but Abby and I go back inside.The two of us scream and jump as a cat with lightning speed bangs into the end table in the living room, turns, runs under the dining room table, comes back out, and runs toward us again and out the open screen door. We both scream again, hold on to each other, and run back outside. However, my brave and angry aunt stays inside and chases out all the rest of the cats.

Later at home I realize that I have another side to me. I can be free and do what I want. I don't want to listen to my aunt or anyone else. I just want to be me, which is be free of anyone telling me what to do.

I admit that when I'm with my cousin, I sometimes turn into an evil person. And I like this feeling of being bad 'cause I feel strong and powerful.

CHAPTER 10

Maggie

Almost two and a half weeks pass before the ban is lifted from my two cousins being grounded for the cat incident. For me it is indefinite to a degree. My mother stated, "You are never allowed to be alone with your cousins again." This includes trips to the record store. I basically walk back and forth to school, do my job of delivering the newspaper, complete my homework, and take care of chores at night. It isn't too bad. I am used to being alone and isolated much of the time even though it's summer.

I can see from the dirty old window in my bedroom my aunt, my cousins, my aunt's friend Sandy with her kids, and my brother and sister get into my aunt's El Camino and Sandy's big brown car with their towels, shorts, bathing suits, and sandals. They are going to the beach, and I am not invited. As they drive away, I can feel rocks in my throat as I suppress the urge to cry. To keep busy I deliver the newspaper around the neighborhood. When I get to this old, abandoned-looking house hidden back away from a walkway with trees, shrubbery, and unkept grass, I can't figure out where the front door is. As I walk around the house, I come across three doors. I look up, and a face appears through a dirty broken window.

"Hey, you," says a dirty-faced girl with straggly hair. Suddenly she disappears, the front door opens, and out she pops. I extend the folded newspaper toward her.

"Hi, I didn't know which door was the front door. You look familiar," I say as she takes the paper with her grubby little hand.

"It's me, Maggie. Don't you remember me? I came over that day when you all were out on the grass. Remember I can do a cartwheel." In that moment she lunges forward and does the most perfectly aligned cartwheel I'd ever seen up that close.

"Oh yeah, I remember you. You looked different that day."

"Well, my hair's not combed right now. You wanna hang out later?" Maggie asks as she attempts to organize her straggly hair with both hands.

"I have to finish delivering the newspaper right now. Besides, no one is home. They're all at the beach."

"I could help you deliver the newspaper if you want," she says with big brown sympathetic eyes. In an instant I feel those eyes absorb my loneliness.

"Sure, if you really want to," I respond shyly.

"Okay, be right back. Lemme go ask if I can go," she says as she trots into the house.

I wait and wait, about five maybe ten minutes, and she does not return. Therefore, I muster up the nerve to knock on the door. I knock and knock, but no one comes forth. On one final knock, the door falls open slightly. As an unknown guest, I go inside. I stand in a small dingy square room with two closed doors. The paint on the walls is yellow and peeling. I look to the ceiling and notice the antiquated cornice that reveals a once fine, grand place. There is no furniture in this little square of a room. As I turn to look at the broken window, one of the doors opens abruptly, and Maggie emerges. She quickly closes the door behind her, and I am not able to see what is on the other side.

"Hi, I was knocking, and the door opened by itself."

"It's okay, I know," Maggie smirks. "It does that sometimes. My dad's been saying he's gonna fix it. Hey, you, I can't help you with the newspaper today because me and my brother are gonna be picked up. We have to go help Uncle Jack. But my dad says I can go over to you guys tomorrow."

"Okay, come over in the morning. I'll tell everyone," I say excitedly.

She smiles and waves goodbye as I wave back and depart on my journey to deliver the paper.

CHAPTER 11

My Aunt's Pool

Ding-dong, ding-dong, ding-dong rings the bell at the front door as I open my eyes from sleep. I look at the clock. It is 7:50 a.m. Who could be at the door so early on a weekday during the summer? I slowly get up, wrap the blanket around me, and go to open the door.

"Hey, you. You still sleeping?"

"Hi, Maggie." I exhale with half-closed eyes. "Forgot you were coming over. You wanna come in?"

"Okay," she says with a sheepish smile.

"I gotta get ready. Here—I'll put the TV on while you wait."

"Okay. Where's everyone else?" she asks quietly.

"They're still asleep. I'll see if they wanna get up." I head into the bedroom. As I get dressed, I attempt to wake my brother and sister; however, they don't want to rise. They had a long day at the beach yesterday, and I forgot to tell them Maggie was coming over today. Therefore, I go back out to Maggie alone.

"My brother and sister don't wanna get up. They came home late from the beach yesterday."

"That's okay," responds Maggie.

"My cousins next door are still asleep too," I add.

"That's okay," repeats Maggie.

I sit on the chair that faces, on an angle, the couch where Maggie sits. As I stand to lower the volume on the TV, I say, "You know I really wanted to go to the beach yesterday, but I wasn't invited. My aunt doesn't like me."

"That's okay," responds Maggie reassuringly. "I've never been to the beach or even in a swimming pool."

"Really?" Suddenly I'm at a loss for words. My shyness overtakes me. I realize that it's just me and Maggie in a quiet, intimate setting. My eyes fix on the side table with the lamp. A ray of sunlight pours in alongside the closed curtains and shines like a spotlight on part of the table that the doily does not cover. I know what doilies are because my mom has them all over her house.

I focus on the dust that swirls into the light before I say, "Do you wanna get in that aboveground pool that's on the grass by my aunt's house?"

"Is it your aunt's pool?" asks Maggie cautiously.

"Yeah, but everyone gets in it. It's just that she's still asleep so we gotta be quiet," I explain. "Besides, I'm the one who filled it so I don't think she would care. She said the pool was for all of us."

"Okay, but I don't know how to swim," Maggie says.

"That's okay. The water is really shallow. All you need is a bathing suit. Do you have one?"

"Yes, I'll run home and put it on," blurts out Maggie happily.

As Maggie heads home to change and I put on my swim trunks, I think it odd that she owns a bathing suit when she's never been to the beach or in a pool. Maybe she uses the bathing suit in the bathtub and pretends to be in a swimming pool.

It's not long before Maggie returns in a plum-colored bathing suit with an off-white towel wrapped around her. "Okay, I'm ready!" she says excitedly.

I take a deep breath and put a finger to my lips. "Shhh, you've gotta be really quiet out there by the pool. And when you get in, don't splash the water around. It's gonna be cold at first, but it feels good after your body is under the water."

Maggie nods her head in agreement. My heart beats fast as I take her hand, and we quietly and slowly walk toward the pool. She is on her tiptoes. The pool is sparkling blue and causes a wave of excitement to rush through me. "You go first so I can hold the ladder," I whisper. "Someone has to hold it 'cause it falls to one side."

Maggie nods okay, climbs to the top, and stops as I hold the ladder on one side with both hands. She takes in a deep breath of air and lets it out. "Are you sure I won't drown?"

"No, it looks deeper than it is. Just go in slowly," I whisper.

"'K," responds Maggie.

Surprisingly she slips easily into the pool with her arms raised above her so they don't touch the water. It usually takes me a while to jump in like that. I put my feet in and sit on the highest step of the ladder. Then I go down the next step to get in farther and so on and so on until I adjust to the cold water.

"I know it's cold, huh?" I ask.

Maggie starts to respond, "Yeah, but it's nice, I ..."

We are suddenly distracted by a loud, wood-crackling sound. A side door with a shade pulled down over the glass panel cracks open. It's the doorway to my aunt's bedroom, which is hardly ever used.

"Get out of that pool, right now!" commands my aunt. She looks frightening and ghostlike in a white nightgown with huge, messy hair. She walks down the two concrete steps and takes a few steps forward until she is standing in the grass. Maggie is frozen and looks like a deer caught in the headlights with her huge brown eyes. Her arms are still above the surface of the water. "Get out right now!" my aunt repeats with an extra puff of air added to the *r*.

"We were being quiet," I dare respond to the scary, overpowering presence of my aunt.

Maggie exits the pool immediately.

"The pool is not ready for swimming!" yells my aunt. Then she points at Maggie with her crooked double-jointed finger. "And you, little girl, don't you ever get in my pool again."

"You're the meanest aunt ever. I hate you," I holler back angrily as Maggie and I start to walk away.

"Whose towel is that? Get it outta here!" yells my aunt.

Maggie runs back, grabs the towel, and whispers "sorry" to my aunt without looking up at her. Maggie and I move quickly toward her house.

"I'm really sorry, Maggie. I told you my aunt hates me, but she didn't have to be so mean to you."

"It's okay. She probably has a headache," explains Maggie.

"Well, I'm gonna tell my mom, and you tell your mom."

"Don't worry about it. She doesn't know me very well. Let's just forget about it."

"I'm gonna make this up to you. Me, my brother, and my sister will take you to the Highland Park pool. It costs a dollar twenty-five, but I'll pay for you."

"Okay," says Maggie, squirming. "Just tell me a day ahead so I can ask my dad."

"Deal," I say and reach out to shake her tiny grubby hand.

Later that day I tell my brother and sister the whole story and ask them if we could all go to the public pool, which I call the big pool, with Maggie the next day. They say yes, for sure.

CHAPTER 12

At the Dinner Table

Dinnertime starts a little late this evening. It is about 7:40 p.m. when my brother, my sister, and I serve ourselves plates of lemon chicken spaghetti. My mom is delayed because she is having an important conversation on the phone, and I suspect it is with my aunt.

"Mom, the food's getting cold," I holler.

"I'm on the phone!" she snaps back from the living room.

As we wait, my brother picks a mushroom from his plate and pops it into his mouth. I slap his hand down and mutter, "Wait for grace."

About five minutes later, Mom comes into the kitchen to fill her plate, and our food is already getting cold.

"Where's the French bread?" she asks in a serious tone.

"In the oven," I respond. "I told RJ to take it out."

RJ runs to take it out. Everyone is starving when we finally dig in. No one says anything for a while because we are too busy stuffing our mouths.

Mom finally looks up at me and asks, "Is there something you wanna tell me?"

"Nope," I respond and swallow too big a gulp of food.

"You know what you did with that girl in Sonje's pool today."

"I didn't do anything with Maggie in the pool. We barely got in, and Sonje came out from nowhere and started yelling at us to get out of the pool."

"Quattuor, why don't you grow up? I am sick and tired of putting up with your shenanigans."

"But, Mom, I didn't do anything. I swear!"

"Listen to me good and clear. That girl, Peggy—"

"It's Maggie."

"What does it matter? The point is that girl, Maggie, is off limits to all of you. You understand me?"

"Why?" all of us kids cry.

"She's my friend. She's never mean to anyone," claims my sister.

"Let me finish!" Mom yells and pounds her fist on the table. "That girl has lice," she says through clenched teeth. "And if you've been playing with her, there's a good chance you could have lice too."

"We saw a film about it in school," says RJ.

"Listen, Sonje's gonna empty out the entire pool and clean it," says Mom.

"What's the big deal? If I get it, I'll shampoo my hair real good and kill everything," explains my sister.

"Did you hear anything I said?" snaps Mom as she stares down my sister with wide eyes.

My sister closes her lips tightly into the smallest shape of a mouth she can make.

"Sonje has already gone to that girl's house to talk to the mother. You are not allowed to see her. The little brother has lice too. The whole family probably has it."

"But, Mom, how does Sonje know Maggie has lice for sure?" I ask.

"During Sonje's meeting with the PTA, she found out. That girl is not allowed at school until they check her out once she's treated," explains Mom. "What's important is that you don't hang around with that girl."

"You just don't want me to have any friends. Sonje is the meanest aunt, and you are the meanest mother on the entire planet!" I shout as I get up from the table.

I go into my room and slam the door. I lie in bed and think of poor Maggie. Does she know everyone is against her? Can't she just get treated right away and be normal again? Does she know that we're not allowed to hang out with her? I have to see her tomorrow and explain everything. I don't want her to feel bad. I want her to know that I still care about her, and when she is cured from this lice thing, we can all hang out together again. I think about seeing her and explaining everything to her over and over again until I grow tired enough to fall asleep.

I have the strangest dream about Maggie that night. She and I are walking to the big pool together as we hold hands. Her hand feels tiny and soft. When we get to the park with the pool, we stop, and I turn to look into her big brown eyes. The sun is bright, and I can see that her eyes are a lighter brown around the pupil. She is so pretty, and I feel connected to her as if we have always known each other. It feels good to be next to her, and I want to hug her. Then I wake up. It was such a nice dream so I close my eyes and try to go back to sleep, but I can't. I think about her, but it's not the same as the dream because I'm awake now. I can't wait to see her again.

CHAPTER 13

Maggie's Family

I wake up early the next morning, skip breakfast, and head over to Maggie's house. I knock on the door solidly, but no one answers. I start to walk away but turn around, go back to the door, and knock again. I wait thirty seconds in silence and think of how much I want to talk to Maggie. Then I turn around again and start to walk home with my head down. At this moment I hear the door crack open. Quickly I turn to go back. A woman with greasy, straggly blond hair looks down at my feet. A familiar odor coming from inside the house fills my nostrils. This scene appears to have happened once before. Maybe I dreamed it. This feeling of déjà vu distracts me so I don't say anything. The woman doesn't say anything either and gently closes the door without ever looking up at me. It isn't until I snap out of my dreamy state that I walk toward the closed door and knock again softly. I touch my thumb to my pinky and whisper, "One." Then I touch the finger next to the pinky and whisper, "Two," and then the middle finger, "Three." I feel uncomfortable. Maybe the woman thinks I'm trying to sell something. Although I feel uncomfortable about this next knock, I do it anyway because I know that I can do this two more times because five is my number today. I turn around and start to walk away as fast as I can, and the door cracks open. I turn my head to see who is at the door and trip over a fallen branch onto my side. My two hands go out to block the fall and take most of the shock.

"Are you all right?" says the straggly haired woman in a loud whisper.

"Yeah," I respond, embarrassed. My ears feel hot as I struggle to rise from the ground. My hands tingle with little rocks and tiny bits of sticks smashed into my palms. I walk toward the woman and ask in a low voice, "Is Maggie home?"

"Who are you?" asks the sad-looking, hazel-eyed woman.

"Quattuor. I live about half a block that way," I say as I turn and wave my dirty and hurt left hand toward that direction.

"Maggie's not home. She and her brother are out with their father," the woman replies in a low voice.

"Oh, okay. Well, I'm a friend of hers. Are you her mom?"

"Yep," says the woman. She leans her head to one side. "Aren't you that paperboy?"

"Yes, I've been trying to collect the money for the paper from you all for a while, but no one is ever here when I come by. I'm not collecting right now though; that's okay. I just came to see Maggie."

"Oh, well, since you're here, let me get my purse. You wanna come in for a sec? It must be awfully warm out there," says the woman in a whispered tone.

"Okay," I say.

As I stand in this little room with three shut doors, it reminds me of the Haunted Mansion at Disneyland, and the straggly haired woman is one of the ghosts. She is covered in a thin, white, raggedy nightgown. Her slippers are fuzzy and blue. She opens the door on the right, and we enter a darkly lit room. All the windows are covered with shades and bits and pieces of torn curtains, except for one. Part of the shade looks like it was torn off, which allows beams of sunlight to pour over one end of the couch and part of a chest that serves as a coffee table.

"Have a seat." She points with a shaky hand. "Let me go get my purse."

As she disappears into this dark place, I decide to sit on a firm-looking black leather chair that is ripped in two places on the seat. The couch that she pointed to looks too old and worn out to sit on. The place is nice and cool, but a damp, nauseating odor enters my nostrils. From the corner of my eye, I see a flash of something moving that's white and gray. I turn quickly and see a small boy with a big round head. "Hi," I say. He doesn't say anything but stares at me momentarily with huge eyes and then runs off and disappears around a dark corner.

"I found my purse here; now let me see what I can find in it," says the straggly haired woman in a scratchy whisper as she makes her way to the couch. She places the purse on the coffee table, opens it, and gets back up seemingly startled. She heads over to a high, narrow dark table with cupboards underneath. She opens one of the cupboards and takes out a bottle of some kind and pours a drink into a blue cup. "Do you want anything to drink?" she asks.

"Oh, no thank you," I answer politely.

"You sure you don't want a cold glass of water?"

"No, thank you. I'm fine."

"All righty then," she says and sinks back into the couch. She takes a swig of her drink and pulls out a small coin purse from the big purse, with a pattern of colored cats. Then she lays out change as she counts it out loud. When she gets to eighty cents, she says, "Darn it, I think I've got the rest in here somewhere." She digs into the big purse, scraping the bottom before pulling out some more coins until she has the exact amount. "I hope you don't mind change," she whispers without looking up at me.

"Yeah, that's okay. I can use change," I respond quietly.

She raises the blue cup to her mouth and drains the rest of her drink. She scoops the change with one shaky hand into the other cupped hand and pours all the coins in both of my cupped hands.

"Thanks so much! I didn't bring my receipt book. I'll run home and get it. I just live across the street," I say.

"Nah, doncha worry about it," she says, waving with her shaky right hand.

I hear a door slam from outside, and then a man's voice shouts, "Charlie, Charlie!" followed by a whistle. The big-headed, little blond boy with huge eyes runs out from around the darkened corner and opens the door with both hands. A guy with what my dad calls stubble for a beard and long, dirty-blond hair to his shoulders enters. "Charlie, fold up them two tarps in the yard, and put 'em in the truck," he demands.

He walks into the living room and looks at me and then at Maggie's mother. He has a big nasty mole on the lower right side of his face by his mouth.

"Hi," I say as I put the change into my pocket. I reach out to shake his hand, but he doesn't respond. Instead he walks to the coffee table, grabs hold of the blue cup, and throws it into an empty paint bucket quite possibly used as a wastebasket.

"You and I are gonna have a little chat later, ya got that?" he whispers through tightly gritted teeth as he turns to face Maggie's mom.

"Dean, this is the paperboy. He knows Maggie," she says calmly.

The man looks down at my feet and slowly shifts his eyes up to meet mine. He has the sharpest, clearest blue eyes I've ever seen. "I see my wife's paid you with all her nickels and dimes," he responds.

"Yes, sir. I came by to see Maggie." I turn to look at her mom before I add, "And she recognized me as the paperboy. I told her she didn't have to pay me today."

"The last time I think I paid ya was about six months ago if I recall," says Dean.

"Yeah, I think so too," adds the mom quietly.

"Well, let me give ya at least a couple more bucks," Dean says as he fishes into the pocket of his tight, torn, and dirty paint-stained jeans. He hands me two folded bills.

"Thank you so much," I say as my ears become hot.

"Oh, that reminds me. Maggie … I've gotta pick her up and take her and Charlie to the other house. Then I've gotta pay the phone bill," rambles Dean.

"When will you be back?" asks the mom.

"Don't know," he snaps at her with a sharp glare.

"Well, I put two cans of pork 'n' beans out," she says.

"Yeah, well let's see if you can get 'em on the table this time," he retorts with an irritated tone.

"Okay, I—" she starts to say before he intervenes.

"Just don't be in bed when I come home," he demands. "Is there any of the ice left I bought yesterday?" He walks toward the kitchen, then turns to walk a few paces backward—still in the direction of the kitchen—to view his wife for a response. The mom nods yes as she closes her eyes and opens them, a little too long to be a blink.

"I'd better go. Thank you," I say as I walk toward the door with a slight limp due to my bulging change-filled pocket.

"You're welcome. I'll let Maggie know that you stopped by," says the mom in a low voice.

I feel kind of awkward when I get outside into the bright sunlight. Maybe it's because I wasn't escorted out. I stand outside by the door momentarily and take in a deep breath and exhale before I make my way back home.

In bed that night I review everything that happened. I think I love Maggie. I don't know if she feels the same about me. I just want to see her, but how can I at this time? I love her, and that's all I care about.

Her family is strange, but I don't care. And that odor. My dad used to have that strange smell sometimes when he got home from work late at night and gave me a kiss. It's a sour beer smell. I don't care. As long as I can see Maggie again.

CHAPTER 14

Confessions of a Neighborhood Mom

A week passes by, and I'm out delivering the paper again on a Wednesday. At least the paper is light on Wednesday. When I deliver it on Saturday, the paper is so heavy that it takes me three times as long to get it done. I hear kids laughing as I run up the outside stairs to the open door on the upper-level apartment. The screen door is closed though, so I ring the doorbell. A young woman opens the screen door, and my brother RJ and cousin Hiro jump in front of the woman and say, "Hey, what are you doing here, Quattuor?"

I tell them that I'm delivering the paper, and they introduce me to the mom and their friend Robert, who is younger, around Hiro's age. RJ, who is standing in front of the mom, asks if I want to go to the big pool tomorrow and that Diane, Robert's mom, will drive us.

"Ask Maggie," says Hiro. "Remember you said you wanted to take her before."

"Yes, but you know what your mom and my mom said. We're not allowed to hang around her."

"Why is that?" asks Robert's mom.

"I don't think I'm supposed to talk about that," I say quietly.

"It's okay; Diane is cool. You can tell her anything. My mom says she has lice," says Hiro.

"Yeah, the whole family does," adds RJ.

At this point the mother invites me in and asks me if I want some ice-cold lemonade. Before I can respond, she pulls out a chair for me to sit down in the kitchen and has Robert get a glass for me from the dish drainer. On his way over to me, he sneezes and sprays the whole cup with his slime. She tells Robert to wash his hands, and she gets up to get me another glass. As she walks toward me, she steps on a small fire engine toy and almost falls. She hollers to Robert and reminds him to keep his toys in one spot in the living room or bedroom. When I take a sip of the lemonade, I notice toys all over the living room floor. There are so many, maybe over a hundred. Mixed in with the toys are wadded-up napkins with old half-eaten slices of pizza, chips, empty cups, and even a half-eaten chicken leg on the carpet. I can't tell what the other pieces of leftover food are; all I know is that they are rotten.

"Like I was telling these guys"—Diane points to Robert, RJ, and Hiro, "I respect Sonje for the fact that she is a dedicated mother; however, she is a li'l' overprotective. I think she made that up about that family having lice. She's the president of the PTA, and just because the kids don't take a shower every day, she felt obligated to do something, so she said they may have lice."

"How do you know that she made this up?" I ask.

"Well, because she said something about my own son that I know is not true."

"What did she say?"

"She said that my son's nose is always running and that I should have him tested for allergies. And that I should make sure that he takes a shower every day because some of the parents have complained that he has a BO problem."

"What does BO mean?"

"Body odor," she explains. "I told her that this was untrue. Sometimes my son will wear the same clothes for a couple of days because I don't have a lot of money—I'm a single mom—but he's always clean."

"Well, just don't pay attention to Sonje. For as long as I can remember, she has always been like that. She tries to do everything perfectly and thinks she's all that," I remark.

"The thing is don't go telling your aunt about what we talk about 'cause then she won't allow Hiro or even RJ to come over to visit Robert."

The phone rings, and Diane gets up to answer it. This is a chance for me to take a little break. This woman never stops talking. It seems kind of odd that my brother, cousin, and Robert are in the farthest corner of the living room away from me. I start to walk over there, but there is a pile of toys that blocks me from moving too close. "Why are you guys so far—"

"Sorry, that was Sonje," says Diane from behind my back.

I turn around, and she motions for me to sit back down, asking if I want another glass of lemonade. When I shake my head and say, "No thank you," she pours me more on top of the half-finished glass anyway and brings me a little plate of cookies with an almond in each center.

"What did Sonje want? Was she looking for Hiro?"

"No, she knows he's here but calls every twenty minutes to check on him. She says that's the only way he is allowed to come over. Like I said, she is overprotective. The thing is no one in the PTA ever complained about my son having BO because I asked her to prove it. I said, 'Sonje, if that's true, give me the names of those parents who have complained.' And she just gave me a little smirk and walked away."

"So what if Maggie and her family really do have lice?" I ask.

"Worst-case scenario is if they did, don't you think they would have gotten rid of it already? It's easy to cure. You just buy a special shampoo and wash all your clothes. You see, my ex-husband is an attorney, and I learned how to think like him—you know, in terms of laws and what people's rights are."

"I'm not sure what you mean."

"What I'm saying is Lenore, Sonje, and Sandy used to be best of friends."

"Sorry to interrupt, but who's Lenore?"

"Uh, Maggie's mom."

"I know my aunt is friends with Sandy, but I didn't know she knew Maggie's mom."

"Yeah, well I'm sure you don't know a lot about her. The three of them met through the PTA and were the best of friends. However, when Lenore got a huge inheritance check from her grandpa after he passed away, she asked Sonje and Sandy if they would go away with her for a while to stay on a farm that she bought in Missouri. Sonje turned the offer down right away and said she had family obligations. Sandy, on the other hand, left her kids and working husband behind without any prior notice. There was just a note on the kitchen counter saying that she needed a little time for herself and didn't know exactly when she was coming back."

"So that's what happened to Jon and Alondra's mom. They kept saying for months that their mom was on vacation every time us kids would ask. Then one day she was back like she never left," I say.

"To make a long story short, Sonje has hated Lenore ever since. So that's why she spreads bad rumors about her. I don't think Sandy should have left her family like that, but it's not Lenore's fault. You never know what someone is going through, and it's not like anyone was holding a gun to Sandy's head."

I hear a loud whistle coming from outside the screen door. "It's Hiro's mom," says Diane.

"I know," I respond.

Hiro runs to the door along with RJ. "Forgot to be home at two. My mom's taking me to buy new shoes at the mall."

"You going too, RJ?" I ask.

"Yeah, see you at home."

"I better go too. I have to finish delivering the paper," I say to Diane and look at Robert, who is standing next to them.

"Okay, it was nice talking to you. Come by anytime."

CHAPTER 15

An Apology

Two weeks go by, and I still haven't met up with Maggie. Every time I knock on her door no one answers. The pool was taken down, cleaned, and put away into storage. However, something in the back of my mind doesn't sit right. What if my aunt and uncle got rid of the pool? If they did, it's all my fault. I attempt to distract myself and make a sandwich with a fried egg, cheese, bologna, bacon, lettuce, tomato, mayonnaise, and mustard. It needs another ingredient to make it a combination of ten items. I open it back up and add pickles. Tears run down my face. I am overwhelmed with a great sense of guilt. I ruined a fun-filled summer of joy in the pool with my brother, sister, mom, cousins, aunts, and uncles. None of us ever owned a pool that we could get into at our leisure. And poor Maggie. I destroyed what little joy she had coming over to hang out with us kids. Why was I ever born? If God exists, he should wipe me off the face of this earth. I wrap the sandwich in a paper towel and walk over to Aunt Sonje's house. I can see through the front screen door that the main door is open. I ring the bell, and my aunt asks from afar, "Who is it?"

"It's Quattuor, Aunt Sonje," I say in fear.

"Come in, Quattuor; the screen's unlocked," she says loudly.

I enter and walk into the kitchen. She is washing dishes when I say, "Good morning, Aunt Sonje. I made you a sandwich." The paper towel is wrapped around three quarters of the sandwich, exposing one quarter of it like my mom taught me.

"Wow, that is a big sandwich, and you made that for me?" she says excitedly.

"Yes, I'm sorry for letting Maggie get into your pool."

"I accept your apology, but you didn't have to make me a huge sandwich," says my aunt.

"Well, I wanted to make you the best sandwich in the whole world because I wanted you to know how sorry I am."

"Thank you. It looks really scrumptious, but my tummy is feeling upset right now. Why don't you go ahead and eat it? Why don't you make it for me another day when my tummy doesn't hurt. You just let me know ahead of time."

"Okay, well, I'm gonna go home and eat it then."

"All right, let me know later how you liked it," says my aunt.

When I get home and bite into it, it's already cold. I pop it into the microwave to zap it, and when I bite into it again, it tastes quite delicious. After I finish the sandwich, I take some ice-cold watermelon out of the fridge and slice a big half-moon-shaped piece. After I eat the watermelon, I feel full. I decide to take a walk around the duplex where I live. After my fourth time around, I run into my aunt Sonje walking upstairs to the vacant unit on the second floor.

"Hi, Quattuor. How was the sandwich?"

I turn my head upward to her. "It was really good. It was the best sandwich I ever made."

"Come up with me if you want. You can keep me company."

I catch up to my aunt, and we enter the empty premises where my other aunt Mirna used to live. Sonje takes a tape measure from the kitchen counter and asks me to hold one end while she pulls it out and measures the space between the windows.

"Do you have anyone to rent this place yet?" I ask.

"Not yet. I gotta have this place painted first. Then I'm gonna put out an ad."

I hear the back door open noisily followed by my cousin Abby's loud voice. "Mom, are you up here?"

"In here, Abby," responds my aunt.

Abby pops into the dining room where we're standing. "Claudia called and wants to know if you can babysit Laura on Monday."

"Okay, thank you. Now young lady, come here," demands my aunt. Abby takes a few steps forward and stops with about four feet between her and her mother. "I'm gonna need your help with painting this place."

"No way! I don't do labor. Tell Hiro to do it!" snaps Abby.

"You know your brother's too young to paint."

"Well, then ask Dad," she commands with fluttering eyelashes.

"Don't be silly. You know he works," she says in a throaty, authoritative, nasal voice.

With her head leaning to one side and her tightly wrapped, Jordache-jeaned hip jutting out to the right, Abby stares at her mother with the widest-eyed look she can give. "I can't do it. I can't stand the smell of paint. It makes me throw up."

Aunt Sonje throws up her arms. "Oh well," she says, her mouth forming a hard, tight line.

Abby rolls her eyes, takes a deep breath, and exhales loudly before she turns on one foot and marches away. "Bye, Quattuor," she shouts from afar.

Aunt Sonje turns to me. "Quattuor, can I hire you to help me paint?"

"Okay, I'll help you."

"Thank you so much. Can you start right now?"

"Yeah, okay," I say as I shrug my shoulders.

My brother and sister and I are always ready to help others. That's just the way we are. If someone asks for help, we do it without any questions. I don't know if my mom or dad taught us this; all I know is that we help others if they ask for help. On the other hand, I noticed that my two cousins are quite the opposite. They don't help anyone who asks for it. One time my mom asked Abby if she could help her bring in the groceries after work because none of her kids were around, and she replied, "Sorry, I don't do labor."

I believe my aunt realizes this so that's why she asked me to help. She has relied on me in the past to go to the Hi Ho market for her and do other favors when her own children would not. I believe my aunt realizes that anything I say I'm gonna do, I do.

Back to my aunt and her response: "Well, you're gonna need to put on some old clothes that you don't mind getting paint on like coveralls."

"Okay, I'll go change and come right back."

"Thanks a whole lot," Aunt Sonje says with a swift little smile.

CHAPTER 16

Illuminating Lights

It's dark now, and there are kids playing across the street. I see bright strips of light shine quickly in the dark from over there and go outside to check it out. I see kids running back and forth. I see others with sticks who are screaming and chasing each other. I walk over and say hi to all who can hear me; I never raise my voice.

One of them stops and says, "Hi, paperboy."

He is a big-eyed blond boy. This must be Maggie's younger brother. "Hey," I say.

Before I can say anything else, Maggie shows up and says, "Hey, you," under a bright light of fire from the sticks.

I say hi, and she hands me a stick lighted with fire. Everyone is playing "London Bridge Is Falling Down." It's in the middle stages, and everyone gets fired up when this one guy falls flat on his back while going under the bridge of human arms.

"What's going on?" I ask Maggie.

"My dad showed me how to do torches. He says it's safe and a way to have fun."

"Cool," I say.

"You're supposed to pass your stick around," she says. "Give it to someone else, and they will give you theirs later. Then you have to go under the London bridge."

"Okay." I give my lighted stick to someone who comes to get it, and then someone momentarily replaces it. I'm not sure how this game works, but I don't care.

"Maggie, can we talk?" I ask, and she nods her head yes. I take her hand and walk us over to the curb and sit down with her facing the street, which doesn't get many cars. "I wanted to say that I like you a lot. I've liked you since the first day we met. If you want to go back now, then go, but I had to tell you this 'cuz I think about you a lot."

Maggie looks at me with her big brown eyes and says, "I like you too, but I have problems with my family. You have a normal family and I—"

I cut her off and give her a French kiss. I think it's a French kiss even though I didn't use my tongue. Her lips are so soft and wet, and I feel butterflies in my stomach. "Can I kiss you again?" I ask. And when she just looks at me with those big brown eyes and doesn't say anything, I kiss her again. This time I put a little tongue into it, but it doesn't feel natural. "Sorry," I say. "I don't know how to kiss."

Suddenly she kisses me back with her soft lips closed on mine, and I feel her smooth tongue touch mine. It makes my body tingle all the way down to my feet, and I kind of feel dizzy at the same time. I can't believe what a beautiful sensation this is.

A loud siren goes off while we are kissing, and I see flashing red and blue lights. The cops pull up and approach everyone and announce in a loud speaker, "Everyone who has a lighted torch put it out and drop to the ground with your hands behind your back. I repeat, everyone who has a lighted torch put it out and drop to the ground with your hands behind your back!"

The cops start to pick up all the kids off the ground who had torches in their hands until Maggie's dad comes out with Maggie's mom and pulls the cops to the side in private. Right after that the cops allow the kids to get up from the ground and leave.

"You're the best, Mr. Dad," says one guy.

"Yeah, well you all better get home now before they come back. No more torches!" he shouts.

Everyone leaves. I say goodbye to Maggie and add, "Let's meet next weekend at six at night at your place." She nods her head and gives me a peck on the cheek with her soft lips before I head home. I would have suggested meeting the next day, but I can't because I'm sure my aunt and mom would find out that we were meeting when they said to stay away from Maggie and her family. If fact they are likely to find out that we met tonight, so I have to be patient and careful about us getting together.

CHAPTER 17

First Week of Junior High

Summer has come to an end, and tomorrow is the big day when I start junior high. After I go through my counting routine to help me sleep, I have a nightmare:

> I sit in a huge circle on the carpet with all the rest of the kindergarten students. My arms are crossed as I listen to what Ms. Bronson, the kindergarten teacher, is saying. "A, B, C, D, E, F, G ... Now repeat after me, Quattuor, A, B, C, D, E, F ..." My heart starts to race. "What is the sound for *A*?" My whole body locks up, and I can't move or speak. This doesn't feel right. "Quattuor, repeat after me: the sound of *A* is 'ah'." I remain frozen. The more she talks to me, the stiffer I become. I am trapped inside my own body. My ears start to get hot, and my shoulders become even more

uncomfortably stiff. She lets me be and calls on someone else. After the lesson, Ms. Bronson excuses everyone one by one. Whoever is sitting quietly gets to go outside to play first. "Quattuor, you may go," she says. However, I don't move. I can't. Eventually everyone is excused to go outside, and I remain completely still with my legs crossed on the carpet. A part of me screams in my mind, *Move, you're making everything worse*, but then my stubbornness takes over and says, *No, don't give in; you're too strong for that*. I feel a lump form in my throat but don't even dare think of crying.

When I open my eyes, it is dark and I'm in a cold sweat. The alarm rings loudly in my ears until I get up to turn it off. Gosh, what a nightmare. I rush to get dressed alongside my brother for our first day back at school. My stomach hurts. I'm excited but even more nervous. My cousin Abby promised that she would walk to school with me the first day. Although we are the same age, she has gone through all of this before. I was held back one year in kindergarten for not talking. The teacher didn't know if I learned anything.

When I go to get my cousin next door, Aunt Sonje opens the door. "Good morning, Quattuor. Abby's still getting ready. Let me go rush her. It's getting late."

I look at my watch and start to worry because it's already 7:10 a.m., and I don't want to be late on the first day. Eventually 7:20 a.m. shows on my watch as Abby bounces out energetically with puffy, shiny, wavy hair. "Okay, let's go," she says.

We walk at a fast pace while she talks her head off. She talks about this friend, that friend, her boyfriend, and advises me on who to hang out with. When we get midway and pass by the Alves's house, I slow down and tell her that I'm really nervous. "You look worried. God, your eyes are so big. Relax; loosen up. It's only junior high."

I take a deep breath and start over again, stepping into the next square of the sidewalk without touching the lines. This signifies my new beginning. I do loosen up a bit once we make it to the park, which is before the water and power building, and then the school. "Oh my God, it's Maria Padilla," shouts my cousin. The short, slightly heavyset, auburn-haired girl runs toward us in her black Hush Puppies.

"Abby, que paso? You didn't call me the whole summer. It's so good to see you."

"I know, sorry. I was grounded for half the summer, and the other half I had to go on a family vacation to Pismo Beach and take boring tap-dance lessons," remarks Abby. "My mom thinks I can be a famous dancer."

They continue to talk and walk slowly. It's five until eight, and I tell them that we're going to be late.

"It's okay. It's the first day. It doesn't matter if you're a little late," says Abby.

Maria tells Abby that she still has to stop by Bridgette's. She promised to walk with her the first day. My cousin agrees to go, but I don't and run the rest of the way to school. I make it exactly at eight o'clock and am stuck in a crowd of students looking for their names posted on lockers or where to go to pick up class schedules.

Once I find my homeroom, I am much calmer. It's exciting to hear Ms. Winters, our homeroom and science teacher, speak with her Southern accent. She is black with really long nails, about eight inches long and curled down on her left hand and about two inches long on her right hand. It seems like she really cares.

Before the end of the week, we go on our first field trip. This school, the Learning Center, is a small school within the junior high school. It is designed for students who want a higher education beyond what the district requires; therefore, extra activities that go beyond the classroom are added. We go on a hike in the Angeles National Forest. We follow a trail that starts near the JPL. My goal is to finish first. I run past others, jumping on rocks through small streams and rivers. There are about five ninth graders I can't catch up to. They say mean things to me, such as "Come on; catch up if you can," "Stop following us," "Seventh grade freak," and "Get away from us, weirdo."

When we hit the bottom of a hill, the trail separates into two parts. The ninth-grade clan darts up the hill while I take another trail over a stream where it dead ends. I hear some of them in the distance shout, "Hey, guy, you're going the wrong way."

I don't believe them. I think they're playing a trick on me, but then I notice that they don't follow me. It isn't until the quietness of the forest surrounds me that I turn around and run up the hill. Then I see them from far away. Eventually I reach the end where there is a huge pond. The other guys approach me, and one says, "You took the wrong trail, dude"—he slaps me on the back of the shoulder, "but you made it."

I say, "Yeah," as I look down into the water and notice a lot of giant koi swimming around.

The other guys skip rocks as I explore the beauty of the green trees. About ten to fifteen minutes pass before another kid comes running up from the trail. He is a seventh grader from my homeroom. He tells me that he could have made it to the pond a lot earlier but decided to help Ms. Winters over the river rocks. I like that he is a nice guy and instantly become his friend. His name is Manny.

Many others now arrive, including Ms. Winters, who is patting her head with a handkerchief. "Ms. Winters, you made it," I say.

"Yes, I had trouble getting across some of the streams. Don't think I would have made it if it weren't for Manny helping me balance on those boulders in the streams and rivers. I even broke one of my nails."

She shows me her right hand, and I see the short and jagged pinky nail. "I'm sorry to have run ahead, Ms. Winters. I should have stayed behind and helped you."

"That's okay. It's my own fault for not keepin' myself in shape. Just hope you're enjoying your time here," she says while still catching her breath.

As I walk with my new friend, Manny, away from the trail but still in view of the pond, I think about our teacher, Ms. Winters. She is so nice, and it is so easy to talk to her. I conclude it's because she laughs easily, doesn't ask me a lot of personal questions, and has a real joy for life. Meanwhile, Manny talks about his classes and about how he recently moved from Austin, Texas, his hometown, and about how people always judge him because he's skinny and wears glasses. I feel complete and just good about myself. Almost all my fear is pushed deep down within me, down enough so I feel comfortable around everyone. My body feels strong and good, and I walk with confidence. Suddenly two ninth graders approach us. One of the guys is the one who slapped me on the shoulder when I first got to the pond. "Hey, you two nerds, you're supposed to stay near the pond. We're gonna leave!" yells the shoulder-slapping one.

My insecure self quickly resurfaces, and Manny and I walk back to the swarm of students. As we walk back, I think about how that guy called me a nerd. I will not forget this because it reminds me of elementary school when those bullies picked on me. If he slaps me again on the shoulder, I will hurt him. Once Mr. Martinez, the social studies teacher, and Ms. Winters do a head count, we head back down the trail. And my new friend, Manny, and I and the surrounding gnats make our way down the trail together.

CHAPTER 18

A Realization

My body has gone through a number of changes during seventh grade that I still cannot decipher accurately. What I do know is that I'm no longer the boy I once was. Now that I'm in seventh grade, classes are a lot harder. I need to focus more on my homework, so I'm thinking about giving up my job as a paperboy. However, if I give up my job, I will not have any extra spending money. And it's getting harder to collect money from the neighbors. They either are not home or don't want the paper anymore. I think about this as I start to collect on my route. As I approach Maggie's house, I notice the windows are all boarded up. I quickly knock on the door, but no one answers. I count to five and knock again. I repeat this ritual of knocking four more times with five-second intervals, and sadly no one answers. I hope Maggie and her family didn't move away.

I walk to the next house of a rich old lady, Ms. Johnson. Her daughter opens the door and tells me that Ms. Johnson is resting and doesn't feel well today. She closes the door while she goes to get the money. The door opens a few seconds later with Ms. Johnson, shielded by the screen. She usually doesn't open up the screen when I come to her door. She says it's too chilly to come outside no matter what the temperature is. It's like talking to a silhouette. She informs me not to deliver the paper for two weeks because she will be out of town. However, she gives me a large tip of three dollars and asks me how everything is going. I give a superficial response of "Fine, and you?" She tells me that she had pneumonia. Although it has cleared up, it left her in a weakened state, so her daughter agreed to come and help for a few days with chores and grocery shopping. Then she asks me to do her a favor and keep an eye out for any suspicious activity near her property when I deliver the paper to other houses on her street while she is out of town.

"Yes, of course I will, Ms. Johnson. Speaking about suspicious activities, do you know anything about the house to the right of you? You know the one that you have to walk down that path in back of all those trees. I went to collect for the paper and noticed that all the windows are boarded up."

"I do. They got evicted. There hasn't been anyone there for 'bout a week now," says Ms. Johnson.

I thank Ms. Johnson and wish her a great vacation as I proceed on my collection route. It angers me that all this time has passed and I didn't even know that Maggie and her family moved out. They've always had this distant secret life that I could never become a part of. Maggie and her brother didn't even go to the same school I went to. Their parents supposedly didn't want them to go to any school in the district that temporarily kicked them out for having lice. Instead they went to some other school in a different neighborhood with their cousins. Nothing will ever be the same again. Maggie is gone. I only have one friend at school now, Manny. Although I have my brother, sister, and cousins, it's not the same. They all have their friends, and I only know them vicariously.

The next place I stop by is the apartment building where Ms. Ramirez lives. Ms. Ramirez is a good-natured soul. She tutors kids around the neighborhood for a small fee from their parents. "Hi, Quattuor; come in," she says as she opens the door upon my fifth knock.

I eagerly enter her small place and look at her iconic figures of Jesus, Mary, the wise men, and others. They're fascinating to look at because it provides me with a sense of peace. Occasionally she'll have a new edition added to the mix. "Here, have a Dr. Pepper," she commands as she grabs one from the fridge.

Her three-hundred-pound frame barely fits through the narrow passageway to the kitchen. She moves a partially knitted string of yarn off a chair and motions for me to sit as she sinks into her favorite chair next to me. It seems awkward because her place is small. She tells me how she's knitting a sweater for Karla, her daughter, while she's away for a month in Maine with the church. They're helping raise money for the poor.

"And Luis"—her son, "how's he doing?"

"He's at boot camp in the Marines," she says.

"Wow, you have a great son and daughter. They do everything right. I hope I'm like them when I get older," I say and pout.

"What's wrong? You're talking to me, Ms. Ramirez. I know when something is bothering my Quattuor."

Knowing that she will not back down, I give in to what I'm feeling. "I guess I really don't like the school I go to."

"You survived last year in elementary school. What's going on in junior high?" she asks.

"A lot. I only have one good friend at school. And everyone is so smart. I don't understand my History and Math classes. These teachers don't explain anything right. I just wish it was summer so I could hang out with my cousins and friends in the neighborhood."

"Let me ask you: Do you have a favorite teacher?"

"Yes, Ms. Winters."

"What does Ms. Winters teach?"

"Science and calligraphy," I state.

"Well, you get to know Ms. Winters well and give her an extra hand when she needs one. Junior high can be tricky to get used to. Just focus on the good for right now, and everything should start to work itself out," she advises.

When I leave Ms. Ramirez's place, I feel a little relief but still sad. When I'm halfway down the block, I hear Ms. Ramirez call my name from afar. I turn and walk back, and she gives me the money for the paper I forgot to collect; then she gives me a hug. "Good luck," she whispers in my ear.

It was hard not telling Ms. Ramirez what was really bothering me the most: the loss of Maggie. I couldn't say anything though because I know she would tell my mom and aunt and I would get into a lot of trouble.

CHAPTER 19

Survival of the Fittest

A year goes by, and I am now in eighth grade with the same good friend, Manny. The difference this year is that I have acquired some enemies. It started with minimal teasing one day during history class. Every time the teacher asked me a question and I answered, this one boy, Allen, said my name in a teasing, long drawn-out way. "Qua ... t ... t ... u ... o ... r."

It's as if the teacher was in on it because everyone could clearly hear this kid. The other students in class laughed, and Mr. Contreras asked me another question when I'm sure he could see what was happening. Then I noticed a brief smile come from Mr. Contreras as he looked down to the ground.

The next day I see Allen outside with his group of friends, and he says, "Qua ... t ... t ... u ... o ... r," and everyone around him laughs. I am with Manny, and this only makes matters worse because he gets teased too. Allen says my name in that teasing way, and someone from the hooligan group says, "Oh, look who it is: the little four-eyed Texas freak boy."

"Shut up, you guys. Go find something to do with yourselves. Leave us alone," says Manny.

"Ooh, tough guy, is that all you got to say?" someone from the group says.

Manny advises me to just ignore those jerks. I do by pretending they aren't there. Then one day, while waiting outside after nutrition by the bungalow steps for the teacher to come for math class, Allen and his friends start their teasing again. This time, however, they shoot paper clips at the calves of my legs with rubber bands. I say, "Stop! Don't do that again," and I go to push Allen, but unlike the bullies in elementary school, they all jump back.

They laugh out loud, and Allen says, "Gotta be faster than that. When Mr. Debon comes, I'm gonna tell him you're trying to start a fight with me."

Mr. Debon shows up, and that's exactly what some of the group shouts. "Mr. Debon, Quattuor is trying to pick a fight with us. He tried to push Allen."

Luckily two girls come to my defense and say, "It's not true, Mr. Debon. You know Quattuor; they're just messing around."

Mr. Debon looks at all of us and says, "Stop fooling around, guys. Remember you're LC students, so conduct yourselves accordingly."

"Watch, Quattuor," whispers Allen as he passes me upon entering class.

It hasn't been all bad though because some of the girls come up to me periodically and tell me how smart and great I am and to just ignore those guys.

One day I'm opening my locker next to this one girl, Rachel, and she says hi and to hang in there because we only have one more year in this school. Then a group of about four of her friends come by, and they all greet me positively. One girl says, "Quattuor, you know who you look like?"

I shake my head.

"You look like Keith Richards, and me and my friends think you're cute, so keep your chin up. Don't let those guys pick on you."

"You're making him blush," says another auburn-haired girl, and they all laugh loudly.

"Thanks, I don't know what to say. You're all so nice and pretty."

They laugh out loud, and one says, "We'll stop embarrassing you now. Have a good day."

I do have a good rest of the day. I feel a little bit happy for once because everything has gone smoothly. I helped Ms. Winters during lunch clean out her cupboards and got an A on a book report that I did on cotton in her class. Later, during horticulture, I taught my group how to properly plant cantaloupe seeds by making a circular mound around the seeds rather than a straight mound that is used for most seeds.

It isn't until I am walking home after school one day that my luck changes. I walk through the park just outside the school and feel something hard hit the back of my leg. I look to my left and see Allen and his hooligan gang about twenty feet away. "Qua … t … t … u … o … r," shouts Allen as they throw little rocks at me.

I start to walk as quickly as I can. After ten steps, if they're still following me, I'm gonna run. If I run, I think they'll chase me, but I will have a better chance of getting away from them. I start to count the steps, but I'm walking too fast and it's hard to concentrate, so I count in a different way. "One thousand one, one thousand two, one thousand three," I say, and then several little rocks hit me below the waist on the back of my legs. Then one small rock hits me in the back of the head, and this makes me react quickly without thinking. I pick up one of the little rocks, turn around, and throw it as hard as I can toward the enemies. It hits one of them, and they start to run toward me as they pick up bigger rocks to throw at me. One hits me in the back as I start to run.

When I cross the street from the park, I run into the parking lot and turn the corner by the Hi Ho market, and someone calls my name from inside the store. It's Elena, and she asks why I'm in such a hurry. I tell her that I'm being chased and can't talk right now. A rock hits her black Hush Puppies shoe and puts a brown mark on it. Everyone in the gang stops by the Laundromat, which is next door to the market about ten feet away.

"What the hell you doing?" shouts Elena. "Who threw this rock at my shoe? You're gonna pay for my new shoes. Who threw it? And why are you chasing Quattuor?"

She walks toward the group, and Miguel says, "It was an accident. Let me dust off your shoe for you."

I follow Elena and say to her, "Come on. Let's go. They're just bullies."

"Quattuor was throwing rocks at us," says Allen innocently.

The guys whisper to one another and laugh quietly.

"You think you're funny. I know what you say about me behind my back in class, Allen," says Elena.

"Well, it's true. Everyone knows it. You're cyclops girl," says Allen loudly, and they all laugh out loud.

Elena gets up real close to Allen's face. He is just a tad taller than her.

"Come on, Elena," I say and grab her hand, but she pulls it away from me.

"Listen to your little nerd friend and walk away," says Allen. "I don't care, girl or no girl, I'll punch you in the face. So back the fuck away." She doesn't move, and he says, "Or should I say, cyclops or no—"

Before he can finish speaking, Elena slaps Allen in the face hard. It's the hardest slap I've ever seen, and it is loud too. "Hit me, bitch!" she yells.

There is a red mark on Allen's cheek, and his eyes are watery. He makes a fist, and his friends pull him back. "Dude, it's not worth it. You could get arrested," one of them says.

They all turn around and cross the street back into the park. "Watch, bitch! You too, Quattuor," yells Allen once they're across the street in the park.

"You wanna know who the freaks are in school? It's all of you, you losers!" yells Elena.

They continue to walk farther away, and Elena and I turn around and walk toward Hi Ho. "Can I walk you home, Elena?" I ask.

She says yes, and we walk without talking. We don't go the way I remember to her house. Instead she takes me to another park on the way. She asks me if I could swing on the swings with her for a while. I gladly agree. This park is small with no one in it. As we swing gently back and forth, she grabs hold of my hand and says that it is more fun to swing back and forth like this. It's a little tricky though because we have to go back and forth at the same time to swing smoothly. But we're able to do it without telling each other how to do it. It's like when we walked to the park. We didn't have to talk. It's almost like we know what each other is thinking and can just feel comfortable being together like this.

"Why do those guys call you cyclops?" I ask.

"You don't know?" she asks. She looks down at the sand, and we rock gently back and forth on the swings.

"No, what is it? You seem so serious right now. You don't have to tell me."

"I'll show you," she says.

She looks at me directly with one eye. The other eye is covered by her long bangs on the left. She's had this same hairstyle ever since the first day I met her in second grade. "What? You're still being serious."

She takes her left hand and moves the left side of her bangs up above her forehead, and there is no eye. There is only a smooth surface of skin where an eye would be.

"You only have one eye," I blurt out.

"What do you think of me now?" she asks.

I take a deep breath because I'm a little bit nervous. I don't know what to say to her. I think I am a little scared because it's different. "Can I—"

Before I can finish, she says, "When I was two years old, I was in a car accident. They couldn't save my eye."

"But—"

"My dad wanted me to be fitted for a fake eye. I wouldn't be able to see out of it, and I said no way."

"I think it's okay like that."

"Yeah, I've seen pictures of what it would look like, and it would look so fake. Besides, I am happy with who I am right now. My mom taught me this."

"What do you mean?"

"My mom says to be happy with what God has given you, because if you are, others will accept you for being who you really are."

"Elena, I'm still a little freaked out, but I think you are a really great person."

"Thank you!" she whispers.

"I know what a great family you come from—a nice home with a steel gate, and a mom and dad who are there for you when you come home and make dinner for you every night."

"No, Quattuor. You walked me home one day. My family isn't perfect. I have one eye because of my dad. He was drinking the night of the accident. That's why we crashed with another car on the opposite side. And yes, he stopped drinking ever since then, but everything is still not right."

"What do you mean, Elena? Your mom is such a good mother; I'm sure it must help."

"Actually, Chloe isn't my real mom. My real mom died in the accident. My dad got remarried to this nice lady, Chloe, that he met at his AA meetings."

"So you've been through hell?"

"Yeah, Quattuor."

We look at each other for a long time. I know that Elena likes me a lot, but I don't share those same feelings for her. I believe she knows this. Like I said before, we kind of know what each of us is thinking without saying anything. Therefore, she tells me to walk her the rest of the way home and that she'll see me at school later. When I'm with her by the black steel gate of her house, she kisses me on the cheek, and I lift up her hand that I was holding on the walk back and give it a kiss.

CHAPTER 20

Swim Meet

Eighth grade was a turning point for me. A year later I decide to use my mom's friend's address and start ninth grade in high school rather than finish junior high. The junior high I had been attending goes from seventh to ninth grade. In the San Gabriel district, however, high school begins with ninth grade. Besides, I want to join the swim team, and there is no swim team at the high school where I live. Successfully I'm accepted at San Gabriel High School.

I feel as agile as ever as I dive off the starting block and glide through the water like a sleek, glistening dolphin. I am able to do the dolphin swim for more than a quarter of the way underwater before I surface and transition into the breast stroke to propel myself forward as quickly as possible. I feel invincible. My robust body becomes one with the water. Everything flows in unison with rippling little splashes as I make my way across the pool. Every frog-like push from my strong legs and pectoral muscles powers my arms and hands against the water, moving it toward the sides of my chest as my head quickly bobs up and down. Coming to the end, I mechanically reach out to grab the edge of the pool. There are two other competitors who have reached the finish before me. What's going on? I felt like I was traveling at lightning speed. How could others be faster than me? Am I that out of tune with myself and my surroundings?

As I pull myself out of the water, I wonder if I'll ever be a great swimmer. I gave it my all. How could this happen? Usually when I try something 100 percent, I excel at it. One of the guys who beat me is supertall. I know some teenage guys have a major growth spurt, but this guy, who is Asian, also has a chest that heaves out with packed muscle. Even his abs are well developed. He looks like he's been working out for years. In any case, I'm angry because I didn't win.

"Good job, good job, Quattuor," says Coach McSwain as he pats me on the back.

I joined the swim team because I believed I was a natural. However, the more I swim in meets, the more I realize that I don't have the edge. I'm just an average swimmer.

I'm in the finals, but because this is a major event involving other swim races and other schools, even from out of the district, our team is done for the day. Therefore, dressed in my team sweats, I decide to rest in the grassy park area. I use my backpack as a pillow and lie under a shady tree. Some of my teammates are napping on the grass too while others are playing music softly, conversing, and/or eating. It is quite peaceful. I feel connected and safe. We are a family. The more I lie here, the more comfortable I become. I become comfortable enough to eventually fall asleep. Suddenly I feel a rough shaking, and I wake up.

"It's time to go," says Shannon, one of my teammates.

I look at her with confusion.

"What?" she says and then giggles.

I follow her to the bus. When I get to my seat, Shannon sits down next to me and says, "Miguel switched seats with me because he wanted to stretch out his legs." I follow her stare and see Miguel lying down on a seat by himself. On the right side of him, Benjie is lying down on an entire seat too. After ten minutes of traveling in silence, I take out my homework from my backpack. Shannon asks what I'm working on. I tell her that I just finished writing a poem for English.

"Do you want to read it?" I ask.

"Sure," she says and greedily takes it from my hand.

Dolphin

Waves break turning lime green to pure white.
The dusty shore holds no life.
A breeze sends chills through my mind,
As I wish to see what I cannot see.
Upon the dive into the eternal bliss of icy waters,
A body like silk, a fin so strong,
Leaves my soul to smolder with glee
As endless time carries us through night,
Under blanketing stars of light that set images
To come forth into a place that's right.

"It's just a rough draft," I add.

"That's okay. I don't know anything about poems," she states. "I can tell that you have great compassion for this dolphin."

"Yeah," I say.

"I like it. You know, I can sense that you have deep feelings for someone. Are you in love?"

"What do you mean?" I think about who I'm talking to. Shannon's a straight-A student.

"Well, it's like you love someone. And I'm not trying to pry in your life by the way."

"No, go ahead," I say eagerly with a slight squeak to my voice.

"Perhaps there's someone you love, and they don't know it. You want to tell them, but you don't think they feel the same way about you. Or maybe you told them already, and they don't feel the same way about you."

"Okay. Then what does the dolphin have to do with all of this?" I ask.

"Let me read the poem again."

"Yeah, sure," I say.

After she reads it again, she holds on to the poem and says, "Maybe you have a love for dolphins, and this dolphin metaphorically represents the one you love. I don't know if I said it correctly but something like that."

"Wow! You're really good at this poem interpretation stuff. You make me seem so smart as if I thought all this before writing the poem."

Shannon doesn't say anything for about five seconds before she turns to me. "You know subconsciously part of your mind leaked out while you were writing your poem."

"You are amazing. I think you'd make a great psychiatrist someday," I say.

"No, a psychiatrist is an actual doctor. I'd have to go to medical school. I was thinking more along the lines of a psychologist or social worker."

"But you're so smart. I feel confident that you could do it," I say.

"Yeah, well they do have a master's in psychology that I can pursue if I decide I want to further my education."

"That's great. You're such an interesting person to talk to."

"I'm glad I sat next to you," she says as she hands me my spiral notebook with the poem inside.

Alondra reaches across the aisle and whispers something into Shannon's ear. I look at her when she sits back down. Her cheeks are flushed, making her freckles much more apparent. She looks at me briefly and then looks down at the ground.

I start to count in my mind, *One thousand-one, one thousand-two, one* … Then I get up and approach Alondra, who is sitting across from us on the other side of the aisle, and I say, "You did great today."

She says thank you and turns away to talk to her friend.

I say, "Just wanted to say that you have the best mom ever who always cheers you and your brother on."

"Yeah, my mom's kind of annoying, but we can't let her down. Thanks, you're so sweet," she says.

I go back to sit down and wonder what I'd be like if my mom and dad were to come cheer me on like that.

When the bus drops us off, everyone is tired and heads toward their cars. "Bye Quattuor," says Shannon, Alondra, Miguel, and a couple of other teammates as I walk to my car. I say goodbye to them too. Wow! I feel great. This is the most normal I have ever felt around my peers. Why was everyone so nice to me? I don't care as long as they were nice. It feels great to not have enemies or haters for once.

CHAPTER 21

A Great English Teacher

A couple of years have gone by with tenth grade the most difficult year because I took too many college-credit classes. I did manage, however, to get into English A for eleventh grade, a more advanced English class. I'm glad I got into this class. It is my most interesting class due to the way it is taught. Ms. Koppell is the greatest and most refreshing teacher. She drives from the Pacific Palisades all the way to San Gabriel High five days a week. She talks about her life a little bit at the beginning of every class. She knows a lot about the latest fashions. She has a Gucci purse and wallet, and other expensive accessories. Her philanthropic attitude about her life and literature make her fascinating. It brings her a special joy and place in society to teach us literature. I wish to live like her someday.

Her interesting story today is that she went to a party at her neighbor's house. She says the place was immaculate and wishes her place was that great. The laundry room was perfect because it looked like it was never used and in mint condition. I want to be rich and carefree like her and her neighbors. I want to have her energy. It's infectious. Her face is old and sagging on the sides like a bull dog, but she is so alive and enigmatic at the same time. Maybe she grew up poor and her lavish lifestyle is new to her. She has the same compassion for literature. When she discusses a piece of literature with the class, the stories come to life for me and every theme, character, and concept swims with curiosity in my mind well after I leave class.

Today's literature discussion is about the short story we read for homework, "A Very Old Man with Enormous Wings," by Gabriel Garcia Marquez. It hit a nerve with me because I could identify with the old man with wings. He was an outsider, and no one understood him. Everyone made assumptions about him and surrounded him. No one tried to be particularly gentle with him. I think the kindest act made toward him was when the priest went into the chicken coup and talked to him in Latin. Another act toward kindness, but not necessarily kind, was when people threw food at him so he would not starve to death.

Ms. Koppell has this casual way of discussing literature. She allows anyone to speak without raising their hand, but when no one says anything for a while, she will stop and randomly choose a student to answer a specific question. If the question is not answered, she will ask another question. If the second question is not answered, she will answer part of the question with an innovative answer and ask the student to answer another question based on part of her response. There are other strategies she uses too; however, I'm only aware of this one.

"Quattuor, how do you feel about how this old man with wings is treated?" I shrug my shoulders. "It can be based on your opinion, or you can comment on how he is treated by one of the characters," adds Ms. Koppell.

I think for a moment as she and my classmates wait patiently. "I don't like how anyone treats him. They assume he is something that he is not."

"If you were there on the outside of his cage with the others, how would you treat him?" Ms. Koppell asks.

"I don't know … I wouldn't throw food at him like an animal. I would look into his eyes and try to search for clues to what he needs. Then I would sit with him until we feel comfortable together. Maybe I'd draw pictures about things that are significant to me and then give him the pencil and tell him to draw pictures about himself."

Stacy, another student, interjects, "I think the same thing. That's sad the way he was treated, I mean—"

"He was suffering. You could tell by his tattered wings," I continue.

Then Mark, another one of my peers, speaks up, "Yeah, well he was very old, and no one knew for sure what kind of creature he was. Maybe he came there to die. I think they just needed to let him be alone. If he wanted something, he'd find a way to ask for help."

The discussion continues, and I feel warm and good inside. I am a part of this class, and everyone is so nice. Why can't I be like this in other classes? One thing I know for sure is that in my other classes, I'm rarely called on to speak.

I wish I could stay in this class all day. I have that same kind of connection with this English teacher that I do with others. For instance, remember Elena? We kind of knew what we were thinking and didn't need to speak. I feel the same way with Ms. Koppell. We don't need to speak about everything. She gets me, and I get her. I know when to ask a question and when not to. I know who to get into a group with. She never has to tell me who to go with in a group because I know what she wants. I also know when she is in a good mood or a bad mood. She is mainly in a good mood. I know she is going to give me a good grade because I respect her a lot.

CHAPTER 22

Senior Year and Graduation

After eleventh grade, senior year passes by quickly. Graduation day is approaching soon, and mostly all I think about is what life will be like once I get out of high school. No more limitations—I can finally be free to pursue my dreams. I can get a job, go to college, and move into my own place so I can come and go as I please. I can finally shape my life into what I want it to be. I can buy furniture and decorate my place the way I want it. As I continue to ponder my graduation and future, I make a sandwich at home. I toast the bread this time, which is different from the past, so that is number one. Then I spread on the mayo and mustard, numbers two and three. I add the fried egg and bologna, numbers four and five. I add cheese, number six. After that I add pickles, number seven. Then there's a slice of ham, number eight. Finally I add lettuce and another slice of bologna, nine and ten. The recipe has changed but not the count. This makes me feel calm when I make this sandwich, especially when I eat it.

As I get ready to go to graduation practice, I stop thinking about the future and think about my senior year. If I could go back in time, I would go to prom because I missed my prom and regret it. I didn't have the nerve to ask anyone and didn't have the nerve to go alone. I could have at least tried, even though my heart wasn't into it at the time. I could have chosen five girls to ask, and if they said no, I would cross them off my list and never think about them again. I couldn't do ten because that would be too challenging. I don't know that many girls. I could have changed it up a bit and asked some of the guys I know if they were going with anyone and just go with them as a buddy; however, something tells me that it would not have turned out well. I gave up too easily, and now I don't have any memories of a prom experience to cherish.

Graduation rehearsal is annoying. Everyone moves at a glacial pace, and the sun beats down without mercy. I'm sure my face will be all red and sunburned by the time of the actual graduation. As I look at the field, it makes me sad because there are too many brown patches of grass and other areas where there is only dirt. My shoes are covered in so much dirt that it makes me angry.

Six hours pass by, and it is now time to go to my graduation. My mom is the only one who comes. When we get to the school, tables are set up in the quad where I have to sign in. As I sign in, they ask my mom her name and to sign in too.

"I'm not a student," she reveals. "I'm his mother."

The two attendees at the table laugh out loud. "I'm sorry; you look so young," the guy attendee responds.

"You could pass for Quattuor's sister," stresses the female attendee.

We all laugh. I'm so glad my mom had me at seventeen. This makes me proud of her.

A few hours later, I go through the graduation slowly but surely. It turns out to be better than I expected because the sun did not beat down so harshly as it did during practice. All the teachers and administrators dressed in professional robes, and the events on the agenda went as planned, which made it a special and memorable ceremony. The only thing that slightly disturbed me was receiving a fake diploma. They told me I would receive my real diploma a few weeks later in the mail.

CHAPTER 23

Valentina

After a summer of working at the video store, it is time to start school at Pasadena City College. I'm so eager to start. I have four classes: health, English, history, and plane geometry. All my classes are fun and easy, except for geometry. This class meets every day, Monday through Friday. It is a difficult class for me because all the postulates and theorems are overwhelming. I need a whole semester to memorize them before I can tackle the exercises with ease. I'm not the only one struggling in this class; a quarter of the students are having a tough time too. Therefore, the professor decides to put us in groups. I end up with Arthur, Chelsea, and Valentina. Arthur and Chelsea are also having trouble with the course. They have no idea how to do any of the exercises. They mention that they may drop the class before it's too late; otherwise, they could receive failing grades. Valentina, however, is a star pupil. She understands everything so far about geometry. I am not a total loss. When she helps me, I understand everything because she is a great teacher.

Two weeks pass, and one quarter of the students drop the class, including Arthur and Chelsea. Valentina and I continue to study together, or more correctly, Valentina tutors me. With her help I manage to get a B on the first test. Class then becomes more difficult and requires more study time, so Valentina suggests that I come to her place a couple of times a week to study. I agree, even though she lives far away in Piru. She has a son, has never married, and lives with her parents and sister.

We soon become close friends, and she invites me to a huge birthday party for her son, who is turning three, at Lake Piru. She goes all out. There are at least 250 people there. And there is one of those inflatable contraptions in which kids can jump. Long tables covered with tablecloths are stacked with an abundance of food. The guests sit around the tables, eating, talking, and laughing. Valentina introduces me to many of her friends and family. I end up sitting next to several other college guys. Before I can eat though, Valentina grabs my hand and beckons some of her other college friends to follow her. She whispers something in the guy's ear who is attending to the giant, inflatable Winnie the Pooh, and he has all the kids jumping in it exit onto the grass.

"Come on," Valentina says to all of us. "All of you inside." Reluctantly and cautiously, we adults enter through the open belly of the bear.

"Come on, let's have some fun," she shouts as she jumps up and down as hard as she can on the soft, air-filled surface. Edgar loses his balance right away from the waves created by Valentina's jumps and falls flat on his back. We all laugh and start to jump with Valentina. Edgar manages to get up with the assistance of Mateo, the other college guy. We jump into the air so high and fall back down so drastically that it seems unreal. I never knew something like this could be so much fun. Eventually we start to tire. But it isn't until Edgar says, "I better stop before I lose my lunch," that we decide to get out of the huge inflated bear. I'm about to make my exit too when Valentina grabs hold of my hand and asks me if I would jump with her a little longer.

Once it's just the two of us, we jump up and down fiercely to try to knock each other down. Every time one of us is about to fall we reach for each other's hands. It isn't until she falls that I reach for her arm and pull her up. She splays her right hand against my stomach to shield herself from knocking into me as I hold on to her left hand after pulling her up. We stop bouncing, and we're breathing hard. She looks closely into my eyes before she maneuvers her face toward me and kisses me tenderly on the mouth. I reciprocate the kiss and then hear clapping and whistles from a surrounding crowd I was not aware of. We both blush and quickly exit the bear's tummy. As I make my way down onto the grass, I lower my head shamefully until I feel Valentina squeeze my hand. "Lift up your head," she whispers. "Be brave."

I respond mechanically, and there are more claps and whistles as a path is cleared on each side of us to pass through. Is this how it is to walk down the aisle after being married? It was just a kiss. When we finally make our way to the tables, her dad asks me how I like my burger cooked. I didn't ask for one, but I say well done. He turns over a meat patty on the grill and says, "Coming right up, señor."

Valentina's mom asks me if I want Jamaica, horchata, or a Coke to drink. I mechanically say horchata, my favorite drink. She brings it over right away. Meanwhile Valentina is talking to a small crowd nearby. Her mom goes over, gently takes her by the elbow, and coerces her away from the crowd as she whispers something in her ear. Valentina has a pronounced look as she makes her way toward me.

"What's up, stranger?" she asks.

I laugh, and she does too as she sits down next to me. "After you eat I wanna show you something," says Valentina.

"I'm all yours," I reply.

After I finish eating, Valentina drives me back to her place. She leaves the whole crowd behind, which I think is a little odd.

However, she's paying attention to me, which I like. She takes me to two rental units her dad built next to her place. She asks for my opinion about them being decent quarters for tenants. As she unlocks the door to one of the units, I feel butterflies in my stomach, and my heart races. She shows me the kitchenette, which is small but appealing, with butcher block countertops, a little stove, and a fridge that fits nicely into the corner. I look at the sleeping area. Because it's a studio apartment, the sleeping area acts as a living room and dining room as well.

"It's a nice, cozy little place," I state.

"Feel this bed. It's really comfy," says Valentina. I sit on the futon. "Let me show you how this turns into a bed."

She makes some adjustment on the sides, and miraculously the couch lays down flat into a bed. Valentina roughly yanks hold of my hand and pulls me down onto the bed with her. The butterflies in my stomach get stronger, and I start to kiss her with both of us lying on our sides.

"Put your head down," she commands as I continue to kiss her. One thing leads to another, and we become entangled in an ineffable act of intimacy.

The next day I wake up with a headache. What happened should not have happened. I like her a lot but don't love her. What am I supposed to say to her now? I think she said that she loved me sometime during our intimate time together last night. She suggests that we should go to breakfast and then go to a museum, perhaps. I start to feel bad because I just want to go home. I tell her that I'm not feeling well and that I have to get home and give my mom some money for the rent. I didn't know this was gonna turn out this way. When I leave, she says to not be a stranger. I feel like such a horrible person.

CHAPTER 24

Senior Writing Seminar at CSUN

Four years have passed since enrolling at Pasadena City College. I am now at California State University, Northridge (CSUN). It is my final year, and I'm eager to graduate. My senior seminar writing class is my favorite class because I have met a great group of writers who make the class interesting. Russell, Andrea, Chelsea, and Chris have great compassion for writing and are all interesting classmates.

Russell is a sheriff who works out of the West Hollywood division. His stories are simple with concise and clear plots. The way he talks is the same. I like him because he is a nice guy who listens attentively and has a great sense of humor. He is easy to talk to as well.

Andrea is from South Carolina. Her best short story is about her trials and tribulations with making homemade strawberry preserves on a farm and selling her product worldwide. She gave a slice of a simple kind of life that I have never experienced. Her views are strong and traditional, and I value her opinions about how to deal with any situation.

Chelsea moved here from Oregon when she was five. She loves animals and has ten cats. She is writing a documentary on homeless, sheltered cats and how to save them. I love to talk to her about animals, especially cats. I had twenty-six cats when I was five years old so we share a commonality.

Next is Chris Feichin. I know his last name because he always introduces himself to everyone with his first and last name. Chris is a mail carrier, and he is older than all of us. He is sixteen years older than me and one year younger than my mom. He is open and honest about who he is. He already has a degree in business but came back to school to major in English, with an emphasis in creative writing because his psychiatrist suggested it. He says that he is bipolar and schizophrenic, and his psychiatrist felt that these writing courses would help him cope with his everyday life situations. He is my favorite of the group because he is the only one who does not flake out on our last day after class to meet for happy hour at Acapulco.

At Acapulco I get to know Chris Feichin a lot better and befriend him. He says that he has been different ever since he was five years old. He used to have tantrums so often that his parents took him to the doctor and discovered he was not the average child. He had mental conditions that needed to be addressed. When he tells me this, I tell him that he is the nicest and most down-to-earth person I've ever met, and that I care about him. He replies that he is on medications that put him on the right track, but if he were to go off of them, there would certainly be problems. If fact his dosages need to be changed or a medication replaced with a new one based on the girls he dates. We laugh a lot about this. I think it's the margaritas. Then he tells me about his relationships with the opposite sex, and I tell him mine. These conversations cement our friendship, and he becomes my best friend.

Over the next year I tell him about my problems with obsessive compulsive disorder (OCD) but wasn't diagnosed for it as a child. I knew I was different but didn't know this was an actual condition. It didn't bother him at all though; he would just say that I was a superior person because I could pay attention to matters much better than most others and not to worry about it.

CHAPTER 25

Best Friend Missing

Now that I'm finished with college, I work as a substitute teacher so I can support myself without too much worry. My life is basic. I only have one best friend, the one who is bipolar and schizophrenic. As long as he takes his medications, he is fine.

When I go to his apartment, the front door is open. "Chris, Chris, anybody home?" I shout when I enter.

An altar with candles, crosses, photographs of Jesus and the Virgin Mary, and a Bible is aglow with light from the candles. It signifies nothing other than a devotion to his religion. Lots of melted wax—some candles are almost burned down to nubs—tells me that this altar probably has been burning all night. A tingling sensation creeps up my spine; I know something is wrong. I go into the restroom. The light is on, and the water is running in the sink, so I turn it off. As I go into the kitchen I notice that his keys are on the counter. I become panicky and sedated at the same time. Where is my best friend?

I head downstairs and knock on the manager's door. A short-haired, middle-age woman with an oval face opens the door. "Good morning, do you remember me? I'm Chris's friend from apartment fifteen."

"Yes, sir. How can I help you?"

"Have you seen or heard from Chris today? His front door was open when I got here."

Her husband comes to the door and stands behind his wife. He is a broad-shouldered man of Russian descent, dressed in a bathrobe that emanates cleanliness because I can smell his freshly showered scent. He says something to her in Russian.

She responds in a monotone, "He came by this morning and said, 'Happy Mother's Day,' and gave me a hug." Before I can respond, she starts to cry. "Mother's Day was two days ago."

"Do you remember what he was wearing?" I ask.

"A bright red shirt and short blue pants," she says.

This is odd because I know Chris does not like to wear bright colors. That bright red shirt must be mine. Before I leave her, the husband gives me his card. "Let me know if you hear anything. Call anytime."

I check the street and notice that Chris's car is there. I drive to Santa Monica beach and check the Mexican restaurant about ten blocks from the shore that we last went to. Then I check the beach and walk on the sand in an attempt to sense his presence. It's a feeling I am familiar with when I know someone is watching me. If he is close by, I believe I would know it. I check the pier. There's so many people, but I persevere through the crowds because at this point it is all I can do. I count one and walk in one direction. Then I count two and change directions. I must get up to ten before I stop looking. I succeed in only getting to seven before I leave the pier; therefore, I must look elsewhere before I stop. I walk under the pier (eight) and then go back to the car. I drive down the highway to Venice Beach (nine). I drive by the beach slowly without getting out of the car before I decide to head home. He doesn't like this beach, so it is unlikely that he is here. However, I still have one more place to go before I reach ten.

Back at Chris's apartment, I call his parents from his small square kitchen table (ten). I explain to his dad that he is missing and that this is so unlike him. His dad, who is a retired detective, says he'll do a search and head down to Chris's apartment tomorrow. I call Cedar Sinai ER only to hear that no one was admitted there by that name. I hang up with a feeling of great despair. This is considered eleven. How can it be? I have totally messed up big time. What can I do? I can't pull myself out of my despair. Then something comes to mind. I open the front door and hop over the little metal strip to land outside with my left foot touching the ground and my right foot still in the air before it touches the ground outside too. Now I'm ready to begin again. I hop back inside over the metal strip with my left foot touching the ground first and take a deep breath. This is the way I'm going to start all over again. As soon as my foot touched the ground and I took this deep breath, it signified a new beginning.

I lie on Chris's king-size bed and know that I have to continue to look for him, but I can't leave in case he shows up. It's only midafternoon, but I'm tired because I only got four hours of sleep the previous night. I couldn't sleep because Chris and I got in an argument that night. He is my traveling buddy, and we were planning a trip to Pismo Beach for a couple of days before he started to act strange. He wasn't himself; he was acting businesslike. His every response was standoffish. He was also wearing my blue and white plaid shorts. He hated those shorts. He would say that they were too long and that I looked like I was in a gang. He doesn't know too much about fashion, so I told him that he was out of it.

I call the wife of Chris's twin brother. I have to call her because the twin doesn't have his own cell phone. I inform Joselyn about what's happened and tell her that I will let them know of any future updates. I want to jump up from the bed and start another cycle of ten to look for my best friend, but I think instead of what I've learned about patience. I remember an incident that I saw in a documentary where a football player and his girlfriend were swimming at the beach. They got caught in a riptide, and the football boyfriend kept trying to swim ashore while the girlfriend floated on her back. The guy could not break through the riptide and eventually drowned. The girlfriend survived and swam to shore after the riptide dissipated. Patience is a virtue. I've heard that women are more likely to be patient and wait for things. With this in mind, I eventually fall asleep.

CHAPTER 26

Chris's Family and the Cops

I'm awakened, startled, on Chris's king-size bed by the sound of two voices saying hello. It is Joselyn and Matt, Chris's twin brother. I look at the clock on the nightstand. It is 7:00 p.m. They tell me that they've come by to look for any clues to help them find Chris. I tell them I've got to get home and feed my iguanas and take a shower. I tell them to let me know if they discover anything. A feeling of helplessness slams me back into a state of sorrow because Chris is still missing. I quickly put on my shoes and wet my hair with water, smoothing it down before I leave the apartment and head to my car. I sit in the car for a while frozen because I don't know what to do. I don't like the fact that Chris's twin and wife are looking through his things. I wouldn't like it if my family did that to me. I think it's an invasion of privacy. If there was something among his personal belongings to help find him, I think I would have known about it. I need a plan. I search my soul and think, *If Chris were dead, I would feel it*. My gut instinct tells me that he is alive. I just have to make a list of ten things to do to help find him.

Once at home I do everything I set out to do except make the list. The peanut butter and jelly sandwich I eat is great because I had to add ten ingredients. I considered the two pieces of bread as two; peanut butter, three; jelly, four; sliced banana, five; crushed corn flakes, six; slice of bologna, seven; slices of pear, eight; thin slices of watermelon, nine; and a piece of lettuce, ten. I sit down to make a list and become sleepy. I'm still worried. I never realized how tired my body can become by worrying and turning over constant thoughts about where Chris might be. I lie down on the bed and doze off.

A little after nine in the morning, I receive a call from Chris's dad. He and his mom are at Chris's apartment. I thank him for calling and rush over to the apartment. When I get there, the front door is open but the front screen is closed and locked. I knock on the screen and shout, "Hello!"

The father opens the door, greets me, and says to come in. I say hello to Chris's mom and notice two police officers taking a statement. The chairs are rearranged in a U shape in the living room, and it is bright, brighter than I've ever seen this apartment. I turn to the light and see that the curtains are open in the kitchen to let in the sun. The whole place has been magically transformed into a nice little cottage. I show Chris's dad and the cops all of the medications that my friend takes. I place one small pill into his mom's hand and tell her that this is an Ativan, which was lying outside one of the bottles on the dresser in his bedroom. The small pill looks gigantic in her tiny hand. She tells me that Matt and Joselyn were there all night looking through everything and checked to see what medications he was taking that could perhaps cause him to lose his memory or worse.

Meanwhile the cops converse back and forth on their walkie-talkies until they eventually announce that Chris has been found. All the blood drains from my face, and I become light-headed as a feeling of elation overtakes me followed by a great sense of relief.

Chris was arrested on Santa Monica Boulevard for obstructing traffic. He was taken to a mental facility at Kaiser. After the cops leave, his dad calls the hospital and learns that his son is no longer there. There was no room for him, so they sent him to another facility in Costa Mesa. He calls down there and is told that Chris cannot be released until tomorrow after the doctor sees him. I offer to pick him up tomorrow, and the dad says that would be fine, but he has to make sure the hospital will allow it because I'm not family. After checking it out, his dad says I can get him, but I need to make sure to bring my ID. Chris's release is set for 1:30 p.m., but I have to call the hospital first to make sure he's ready to be released before I drive down there because there are usually delays. Then Chris's dad calls Joselyn and asks to speak with Matt. He tells Chris's twin the good news and that I offered to pick him up. When the dad hangs up, he says Matt appreciates my offer to pick up Chris but not to feel obligated. If I change my mind, Matt can pick him up, even though he hasn't gotten any sleep.

Later that afternoon I call the facility in Costa Mesa, and I am allowed to talk to Chris. He sounds normal until he says, "Two and four is eight, sixteen and thirty-two is five hundred and twelve, thirty-two and sixty-four is two thousand and forty-eight …"

"Okay, why are you telling me all this? What do you mean?" I ask.

Cnris breaks away from the number counting and says he will be released tomorrow at 1:30 p.m. and to be there at that time. He says not to wait for the nurse to call because it's quite a drive, and he wants to get out of there as quickly as possible. He says it is like a prison with nurses and doctors who won't even let him use the restroom unattended. And because the other patients are supercrazy, he doesn't feel like he belongs there.

"Okay, but what is wrong with you? Did you not take your medications?"

"It's not my fault. The dentist prescribed me medications that were not supposed to be mixed with other meds I take and this caused me to go into psychosis."

"Well, you sound kind of normal," I reply. "Regardless, I'll be by to get you out tomorrow by 1:30 p.m. Don't do anything crazy in the meantime, 'cuz they may lock you up and throw away the key."

He laughs and says, "You don't know how bad it is being here. I'll tell you all about it later. Dang, it is bad! I wouldn't wish this place on my worst enemy."

"Okay, hang in there, love you. I'll see you tomorrow."

After I hang up with him, I think, *He's a little off but not too bad.* I feel confident that he will be good to go tomorrow.

CHAPTER 27

Waiting Area at the Mental Facility

Although Chris's dad told me not to go to the psychiatric facility until I called there first, I start the drive down by eleven in the morning without giving anyone a call. I'm anxious to see Chris and get him out of that place. I get there early, about a quarter to one. This place resembles a hospital, not how I imagined it with padded cells and steel gates under lock and key. The receptionist tells me that Chris is being seen by the doctor and will be released shortly after that. I am escorted to a waiting area, an open space with hard plastic chairs on one side of a major walkway. A woman sitting five seats away from me is repeatedly pulling a rubber band worn as a bracelet on her wrist. I watch as the rubber band continues to snap back each time she pulls it and let go. An orderly comes by and demands, "Let me see the rubber band," to the disheveled-looking woman.

She looks up at the orderly with her head cocked to one side and continues to snap the rubber band against her wrist. "Let me see the rubber band," demands the orderly more firmly this time.

The woman looks at her in a deranged manner for a few seconds before the orderly repeats even more firmly, "Let me see …" There's a little pause before she emphasizes the phrase "the *rubber* band!" She looks up at her again with an even more piercing and deranged look in her eyes. "Well, look at it!" she shouts.

The orderly walks toward two double doors for employees only. She places her card into the slot and punches in a code. When a loud buzz sounds, the doors push open, and she goes inside. Momentarily she brings out another woman, perhaps an RN. "I asked her for the rubber band and—" the orderly tells the RN as she points at the patient and walks toward her.

The RN, not allowing her to finish her sentence says impatiently, "That's okay; let her have it," and turns to go back inside.

"Excuse me, nurse, when can I have a cigarette?" asks the rubber-band lady.

The RN turns around by the doors and shouts, "I'm still waiting for the doctor. I'll ask him again."

"You said that twenty minutes ago. Just get me a goddamn cigarette," the rubber-band lady shouts desperately.

"Okay, lemme go ask him again right now," responds the RN. She turns around abruptly and goes through the swinging doors.

The patient jumps out of her seat, walks a few paces, and leans forward as if she's going to lunge at an invisible being. "Lick my pussy, bitch!" she shouts angrily.

A male orderly from the opposite direction suddenly appears alongside the female orderly whose badge reads, "Rachel." She stands a few feet away from the rubber-band lady. He whispers something into Rachel's ear. "One more outburst and we gonna restrain you again in isolation," says Rachel.

"Okay, but I really need a cigarette. You try to get off cigarettes cold turkey and see how you feel!"

"Jus' sit down right there and watch the TV. If you not gonna do it, you gonna be restrained. Okay?" says Rachel.

The rubber-band patient complies by sitting down. She turns to look at me, and my eyes immediately shift to stare at the TV. I sense that she'll say something mean to me if I make eye contact with her. The two orderlies whisper in each other's ears before they leave the scene. The woman continues to snap the rubber band against her wrist as a janitor comes by with a mop and a dirty-yellow bucket. She mops by our feet and the surrounding area.

"And what the fuck is your problem, bitch? You gotta mop the floor every goddamn ten minutes?" snaps the rubber-band lady.

I have to admit it was a little annoying for this janitor to mop so closely to my feet.

There is a fine line between me being here in the waiting room and being on the other side as a patient in this psych facility. I could easily be committed. I feel that if you don't seem normal, you could easily be committed to this place. If I were to take the lady's rubber band away from her and snap it ten times, I feel that could put up a red flag for me to be taken behind the closed doors of this mental facility. It makes me sad to think that anything slightly outside the norm is judged so harshly. Any credibility I have could be stripped away within thirty seconds. I also feel that being different is like a crime in our society. So many of us judge each other harshly just because we're different. If we could become more civilized and allow for a great spectrum of differences, a lot more people would get along much better. I feel so alone sometimes because I know that I don't think like most people. And this place makes me feel constricted, and I think I may be panicking a little.

CHAPTER 28

Check-Out Time

At, one thirty, I go to the reception area of the mental ward to check Chris's status for his release. "His paperwork is being processed right now. Would you like to go in and see him while you wait?" asks the receptionist at the front desk.

"Yes, please."

Moments later, an orderly comes out and takes me into a secure area where we have to be buzzed in. She leads me down a narrow hallway with rooms on the left and right. I can hear someone shout from one of the rooms, "Chain, chain, chaaain." There is a slight pause and then I hear again, "Chain, chain, chain, chaaain."

When we enter Chris's room, it is dimly lit compared to the bright fluorescent-lit hallways. There are two beds on each side, and Chris is by the door on the left. I give him a hug when I see him. He is wearing blue hospital garments. I ask him how he is and if they're feeding him okay. He looks a little on the skinny side. I let him know that they're processing his paperwork, and then he'll be released. He turns to the orderly and says impatiently, "Can you find out what's taking so long? That's why I'm here in this bed rather than in the rec room. I've been here waiting for at least two hours! You think I want to go back in there with those crazy nut cases?"

"They told me that they're processing your paperwork," I tell Chris again.

"How long can it take to do that? I want to get outta here!" he says.

"I don't think it will be that much longer," says the orderly. "I will go and check to get an update."

"This is Annie," Chris says pleasantly as he waves to the woman in the bed next to him.

I'm surprised to know men and women are together in this ward.

She is reading a book and looks up with a little duck-like grin and says hi through half-lidded eyes. She looks like she's been sedated.

"I gotta go to the restroom before we get outta this place," remarks Chris. He presses a button for staff. "Annie's been the only one I could talk to in this God-awful place."

"Yes, he is my only friend here. I hate to see him go," says Annie, solemnly.

An orderly comes into the room. "What you need, Chris?"

"I'm gonna be leaving soon, and I need to use the restroom." Chris follows the orderly out of the room and tells us that he'll be right back.

"Are you getting ready to leave too?" I ask Annie.

"No," she replies slowly.

"Sorry, I was just wondering 'cause you're not in the rec room with the other patients," I say awkwardly.

"Well, they put me in here to be more closely monitored because they thought I might have been trying to kill myself."

"Oh no!" I say. "Why, I mean what happened?"

"I wasn't really. They thought that because I was playing with a strand of my hair, twirling it around my neck, and two staff guys grabbed me and put me in here."

"Oh no! Did you explain that to anyone?"

"Yes. When the nurse came in and told me why I had to be in this room, I told her that I was just bored and playing with my hair. She said they have to take precautions so I have to wait here until I see the doctor; then I can go back out."

"Oh, I'm sorry to hear that."

"It's okay. I've been through worse," she says meekly.

I'm at a loss for words because I feel sad for her, but I don't want her to know this so there is a long pause of about ten seconds before I muster up something else to say. "What you reading?" I ask.

"*A New Era of Thought*, by Charles Howard Hinton," she says as she shows me the front cover. "It's not that interesting. Not my choice. It's one of the few books here I'm allowed to read." She makes that duck-like grin.

"I like to read too. What's it about?" I ask, stalling for time.

"Ah, about the fourth dimension. You know, science stuff," she answers.

"Interesting. If you learn how to switch out of this dimension, you could get out of this place," I say to Annie with a little smile.

Anne laughs out loud and says, "You know that would be great. When I finish reading it, I'm gonna beam myself right out of this place." She giggles.

"Vámonos," says Chris from behind me. "I'm outta here. Let me give my new friend a big goodbye hug," he says as he reaches down to hug her.

She doesn't even get up slightly for the hug as I look down to see if her legs are going to move off the bed. I don't see any bulkiness under the covers where her legs should be. Then it dawns on me. She doesn't have legs.

"Bye, Annie. It was nice meeting you," I say as I shake her hand. "Good luck with everything." I look up to her eyes.

She makes that duck-like smile. "It was real nice meeting you too."

Chris and I walk to the doorway, and we both turn around to look at Annie one last time as the orderly waits in the hallway.

"I would take you home with me if I could. Love you," says Chris.

"Hey, you, don't you worry 'bout me. Ask your friend there. I'm gonna soar myself outta here one day," reveals Annie as she opens her big brown eyes all the way this time, smiles brightly, and waves goodbye with her small hand.

CHAPTER 29

Going Home

At the check-out counter, Chris has to sign forms upon his release. Then we are led to a small room filled with boxes and bags of clothes. The orderly asks Chris what kind of clothes he was wearing when he was admitted. He tells him a bright red shirt and blue and white plaid shorts. The orderly, Chris, and I go through several boxes and bags but cannot find his clothes, so Chris has to settle for supertight jeans that don't fit him. He has to keep the top button open, and the pant legs are way too short. For a shirt he chooses a flannel one, but the sleeves have been cut off and the bottom left side has a large tear in it. He doesn't have a lot of choices. We conclude that another patient who was released must have taken Chris's clothes for his own.

When we get outside, the sun is so bright that I have to squint on the way to the car. I see Chris squinting as well. As we walk toward the car, I get a call from Chris's twin brother. He says that he has kept in touch with his parents and would have gone to pick him up.

He feels bad that he didn't help out. I tell him not to worry and that it's no trouble at all. He asks me how things are going. I tell him that even though Chris was released, I don't believe he was ready to be discharged. "In my opinion I believe he is about seventy-five percent normal," I disclose to Matt as I turn to look at Chris.

Chris is within himself, indifferent to his surroundings. He sits in the passenger seat with his seat belt on and stares out the front window with a blank expression on his face. Matt informs me that he and his wife are headed for Chris's place to stay a few days so they can closely monitor him. They won't be able to get to his place until tomorrow because Matt has to work and Joselyn has to take the kids to school and pick them up. Matt, however, has made arrangements to take a few days off from work.

Everything goes smoothly until I turn on my left signal to enter the freeway. "Stop! You're going the wrong way!" shouts Chris.

"No, I'm not!" I state firmly.

"Listen to me. You're going the wrong way!" shouts Chris again.

"No, I'm not. Just sit back and relax," I say.

"You're going the wrong way," he repeats with a shriek. "I've been driving for over thirty years. Don't you think I know a thing or two about driving? Pull over."

"No! Sit back and shut the hell up, or I'll take you back to the psych ward," I threaten.

Agitation spreads across his face, and he starts to hit his fist into the palm of his other hand to pop his knuckles. After about two minutes of silence, he says, "Why won't you listen to me? I'm telling you, you're going the wrong way. All this time wasted. When you finally realize it, it'll be midnight by the time we get home!" yells Chris.

"I've had it with you. I've absolutely had it! When we get back, I'm gonna tell Matt how you're acting, and we're gonna put you back in the psych ward," I say with a vengeance.

It isn't until about twenty minutes later that a freeway sign indicates Los Angeles, and I point it out. He finally believes me, saying, "Okay, you win. You're right."

I don't want to talk anymore because I'm agitated and tired. I believe we both are, so we sit in traffic silently for the rest of the drive.

CHAPTER 30

Back at Chris's Apartment with Mom and Pop

Palm trees, bird-of-paradise, and other tropical plants cover the front of Chris's apartment complex as I pull up in front. A feeling of normalcy returns to me. The nightmare is over. When we arrive at his unit, the front door is open but the screen door in front is closed and locked. A wonderful aroma of spices and earthy goodness pervade my nostrils. Someone is cooking a wonderful meal.

"Hello," shouts Chris through the screen.

His dad immediately opens the door. "Hello, son. Welcome back!" he says as he shakes Chris's hand.

"Hey ya, Pop," says Chris before he runs to his mom in the kitchen and gives her a long, firm hug.

"How ya feeling, Chris?" asks his mom before she kisses him on the cheek.

I shake his dad's hand. He thanks me for picking up Chris, and then I go to give his mom a handshake too and kiss her on the cheek.

"What smells so good?" asks Chris.

"I'm making your favorite, sausage soup," his mom responds.

"Oh, Mom, you didn't have to do that. I would have taken you all out to dinner."

"Let me show you some of the messages you got," says Chris's dad as he motions for him to come into the living room.

Meanwhile I stay in the kitchen with Chris's mom so she can show me the final stages needed to complete the sausage soup. She pours a scoop of dry white beans into the palm of her tiny hand and says with a throaty but subtle tone, "Add about this much to the soup after you bring it back to a boil. Then lower the flame to simmer for about an hour or an hour and a half. Be sure to check the beans after an hour to make sure they're cooked."

"Okay, thank you so much," I say, "but I thought you and Niall would stay and have dinner with us."

"Oh, that's so sweet of you, but we've been here since early morning, and we've got a long drive back up to Carpinteria. But how 'bout the two of you come up for dinner next Friday?"

I feel bad for Chris's parents because his mom has such bad osteoporosis and his dad has a heart condition. They are in their nineties. They look okay, but I know looks can be deceiving.

His mom clears her throat. "I know my son is in good hands with you," she tells me. "Please inform us of any unwanted changes in his mood."

"Okay, that sounds great. Chris is lucky to have such great parents," I add.

Chris pops into the kitchen and says, "Hey, Mom, we're gonna go pick up my prescriptions. We'll be back soon."

"Okay, dear. Your dad and I are gonna be heading back up to Carpinteria, but I was telling Quattuor that the two of you should come up for dinner next week."

"Yeah, Mom. I wouldn't miss your cooking for the world."

Right, he wouldn't miss her cooking for the world. When he was a teenager, he kicked his mom in the stomach and told her that her cooking was the shits. Okay, let me be honest here because I'm an honest guy. She got pissed off and grabbed him with her nails after he told her that her cooking was the shits. That's when she pinned Chris down on the bed, and he placed his bare foot on her stomach and pushed her away with his foot.

"Gotta run," says Chris as he hugs his mom and gives her a kiss. "Bye, Pops," he utters as he turns toward his dad and shakes his hand.

"Give us a call if you need anything, son," says his dad.

"Vámonos, Quattuor," says Chris as he heads to the door enthusiastically.

This is a rarity for him to walk way ahead of me. Usually I'm the one who leaves him in the dust.

Once we're in the car driving, I suggest, "Maybe I should get your prescriptions for you so you can spend more time with your parents."

"Nah, they've got a long drive home. I'll spend more time with them next week when we go up for dinner," he explains.

This family is difficult to understand. Chris's parents are leaving, yet he leaves before them. This would be so uncalled for with my family. There is taboo written all over this scenario.

"Wait a second. Your mom went through all this trouble to make your favorite sausage soup."

"I'll eat that later. I just wanna grab something now. Pull into the parking lot. Let's get off and eat here."

"I feel like I'm missing something here. Your mom and dad traveled for over two hours to get to your place and have been there probably since the crack of dawn. Then your mom slaves over a hot stove to make your favorite dish, and you want to go to McDonald's," I continue disappointedly.

"Don't push! I just don't feel like eating that right now."

"Well, I'm not eating from McDonald's. I'm gonna eat the sausage soup your mom worked so hard to cook."

"Okay," he says and shrugs his shoulders.

"You're such a cruel person. You should have just kicked your mom in the stomach again and told her that her cooking was still the shits."

He laughs out loud and reveals to me with a serious glare, "I told you that was a long time ago when I was a hostile teen, and I've apologized to her many times over the years."

"Whatever, but can we at least get your food to go?"

"I just want to go somewhere and sit down to eat. Is that too much to ask?" he snaps back furiously.

"Okay, okay, no more arguing," I say as we go into McDonald's to order.

Once we sit down with his meal and my diet soft drink, I say, "The sausage soup isn't completely done yet. I still have to add the beans and cook it for about an hour to an hour and a half. Your mom showed me how to do it."

"Good. You can take it home with you if you like."

"How can you be so cruel? You have a black heart," I say.

Chris doesn't say anything.

"I thought that was your favorite meal that your mom cooked."

"It used to be. It's just not my favorite anymore," he says as he takes a bite of his burger.

"Why is that?" I ask.

"I don't know really. I just don't like it that much anymore."

CHAPTER 31

The Bee

Two weeks pass by, and I feel restless even though Chis is stabilized and almost functioning at a normal stance. Although Chris is my best friend, I wonder why I don't have regular friends. Everyone in my life seems to have not been of the norm, to put it nicely. I take that back. Some of the girls on the swim team in high school I talked to were normal; however, that didn't last long. What matters most is that Chris is a loyal friend. He will always be there for me unconditionally; therefore, to make sure everything goes okay with his recovery, I agree to go on a trip with my uncle Arturo and his partner, Davie. We are going on Davie's catamaran. I ask Chris, and he agrees reluctantly.

"Come on, Chris, get on the boat. Stop complaining; a little sunlight will do you good," I say as we get on the vessel.

The catamaran glides quickly through the water, and the fresh air passes through my hair while we move toward the open sea. What a beautiful world. It's so peaceful and calm out here. The blue of the sea stretches far beyond what my eyes can see. When the boat comes to a stop, Davie and Arturo pull open the ice chest and announce that it's time for lunch.

"Good," I say. "I'm famished!"

Everyone laughs, and Chris adds, "I'll second that."

More laughter. It's easy to laugh out here. I believe the fresh, crisp air makes us giddy. As we sit together eating turkey and ham sandwiches, Arturo instructs Chris on how to fish from a boat.

"Let's just show them when we actually do it," Davie intervenes.

"He's just worried that one of you might snag him with a fishing hook," adds Arturo.

We all look at each other seriously before we burst into laughter.

"Davie's nervous about you all fishing for the first time 'cause when he taught me, I threw the fishing rod over my head, and the hook dug into his shoulder," reveals Arturo.

"That calls for a celebration," he adds jokingly. "Let's pop out the bubbly."

Arturo passes out plastic margarita glasses and fills them while in our grip. "Be careful," he instructs. "These plastic glasses tip over easily."

Davie raises his glass. "To new beginnings," he shouts as we raise our glasses and clink them together.

"It's getting a bit chilly. Where's my coat?" asks Chris as he slips away to retrieve it.

"I need my coat too," I say as I make my way to the main cabin after Chris.

"If you drink enough champagne, you won't need your coat," Davie says jokingly.

As Chris and I rustle through the suitcase for our coats, a bee buzzes out from the luggage. It flies low and lethargically until it lands on the table. We both shout out interjections, and Chris quickly dumps what looks like fish bait out of a jar and covers the bee.

"What's going on down there?" asks Arturo from afar.

"Guys?" calls out Davie with concern.

"We're okay. A bee came out of Chris's coat," I respond. "Go ahead, Chris. Let me figure out how to get rid of this bee."

"Suit yourself," he snaps as he heads up to the deck.

As I look at the bee, it flutters around toward the bottom of the jar but without the speed of a regular, supersonic, fluttering bee. I look for a piece of cardboard or paper to slip under the jar so I can carry it outside and let it go. When I can't find anything in the cabin, I rummage through the suitcase and discover some of Chris's mail. I look to see if any of it is junk mail and find an envelope I can use as a cover for the jar until I get the entrapped bee outside to freedom. I tap the jar in an attempt to get the bee to fly up toward the top so I can slip the envelope underneath without it escaping. However, the bee only flutters around toward the bottom. I peer closely at the bee and carefully lift the jar a bit and start to slide the envelope under the jar. With alarming speed, the flying insect jumps up and down and heads toward the opening I create. I slam the jar down quickly to create a seal with the rest of the envelope underneath. *What a fascinating creature,* I think as I kneel down next to the jar so I'm at eye level with the bee. I look closely at its pulsating body as it flutters its wings in a gyrating motion. In an instant it stops moving its wings and sits at the bottom on the envelope. It must be sick. I've never seen a live bee not move its wings. I don't want it to die I pull the envelope in one direction to get a response from the miraculous flying insect. It starts to flutter its wings again in a gyrating motion; however, it will not fly up to the top of the jar. Instead it jumps up a little and then lands lethargically.

From the bee's perspective, it's trapped in a jar and can't get out. What if it is highly intelligent and is thinking about the fact that it is trapped? If I were that bee, I would sit there like that too because I'd be trapped with no way out.

"Hello, down there. Did you pass out from a bee sting?" hollers Chris from up top.

"I'll be right there," I respond nervously. I jump up too quickly and knock over the suitcase. Clothes with mail and medications litter the cabin floor.

As I pick up the fallen items, the return address on a piece of mail draws my attention:

Annie Wilson
New Horizons Behavioral Center
1941 Echo Lane
San Diego, CA 91204

"What ya doing?" asks Chris as he makes his way down the few cabin steps.

"I'm sorry. I was just about to take the bee out," I say as I look on the table, but the jar is gone. "Ugh, where's the jar!" I shout.

Chris looks down at the ground as the jar rolls back and forth under the table with a piece of mail close by.

"No!" I shout, alarmed. "Where's the bee?"

"I don't know. I think the champagne's gone to your head."

"No, it hasn't. You make me do everything myself. I was trying to let the bee go, and then I got distracted by this piece of mail," I state as I shove it on his chest.

He grabs it and reads who it's from. "Why are you goin' through my mail?" he asks.

"I wasn't. Everything fell out of the suitcase, and I was trying to put everything back," I explain.

Chris immediately goes up deck without saying anything to me with his mail in his hand.

Once I'm back on deck, Arturo says, "Quattuor, we're about to cast our lines. Are you up to this?"

"You mean to fish?" I ask.

"Yes," Davie says. "You guys can watch us if that's okay."

"Davie, I told you they can do this," says Arturo.

"Okay, no arguments from me," Davie replies.

Albert Rodriguez

We are given our own fishing rod, which is great. After about twenty minutes of trying my luck, I catch a fish that has two eyes on one side of its body. Everyone is overjoyed. However, I'm not too happy about the fact that I killed a fish.

CHAPTER 32

The Letter

Chris and I take a break from fishing. I take a ginger ale from the ice chest as Chris sifts through his mail and opens a letter. "Hey, that girl Annie I met in the hospital wrote me a letter," he says.

"I know, so let me see it!"

Chris reads the entire letter silently before he looks up, puzzled. "Did you ever know Annie before you saw her at the place in Costa Mesa?" he asks.

"No, why?"

"Well, she claims to have known you when the two of you were kids."

"I'm not sure. Did she grow up in Highland Park?"

"She didn't mention the city, but she was quite detailed about how she met you," he explains.

"What did she say?"

"Lemme just read you the letter," says Chris.

Dear Chris,

Miss you lots. Hugs and kisses and everything sweet and nice go from me to you. I'm being taken out of this place and put into a nursing home because they need the bed for other patients. It's supposed to be a less restrictive environment. It's stationed somewhere in San Diego. Perhaps you can come visit me sometime.

On another note, your friend who picked you up the day of your departure looks familiar, and I believe he was the paperboy who lived across the street from me when I was a girl. He was a very nice boy who I had a crush on. I know he may have felt the same way about me, but our friendship didn't last long because our family had to move away. If this is him, please tell him I said hello, and if not, please tell him I said hello. He is a nice man, and I was glad to have talked with him that day.

Don't feel obligated to come by and see me. If you only want to be pen pals, that's fine with me too. I get so lonely sometimes, but this new place I'm going to should be much better. Don't worry about me. It will bring me great joy to know that you and your friend are happy.

Love always,
Annie

P.S. Don't go back with your ex, Bridgette. She's no good for you. She'll only bring you despair.

"Wow! I think I remember a girl like her across the street, but her name was Maggie," I comment.

"Do you guys want to try your luck at fishing?" asks Arturo. "We're not catching anything."

"Okay," I say.

"Yeah, sure," responds Chris.

Davie and Arturo put bait on our hooks, and we cast our lines in the sea; however, Chris's fishing line becomes tangled, and my uncle and Davie have to untangle it for him. After about ten minutes of untangling, the atmosphere becomes quiet and serene. I think about the letter Chris read to me as I look at the deep blue water. The boat gently rocks back and forth. It is soothing, but my head gets too hot.

"Put this hat on," says Arturo.

"Are you a mind reader, Arturo? I was just thinking about my head getting too hot."

"Maybe, or maybe the two of you just look like you're getting too much sun," says Arturo as he hands Chris a hat too.

"Do you guys want some more champagne?" asks Davie as he pops open another bottle.

"Yeah, sure," I reply.

"Not for me, thank you," says Chris.

When Davie hands me the glass of champagne, I take a couple of sips and almost go into a catatonic state. My memories cause me to drift back to the past. I see Maggie vividly. She is so amiable. I remember her big smile, large brown eyes, and casual way of greeting me. "Hey, you," she used to say.

Could this lady at the psych ward really be Maggie? My gut instinct tells me it's her, but nothing adds up. First of all, this young woman's name is Annie not Maggie, my beautiful Maggie. Plus this Annie woman has a duck-like grin, and Maggie had a big Colgate smile. And if this is Maggie, how did she go so far downhill? What happened to her legs? After dwelling on this too much, I become disconsolate.

"What's wrong?" asks Chris. "You look like you've seen a ghost."

"I have! I'm looking at one right now," I say due to the fact that he is almost as fair skinned as the Queen of England.

Arturo and Davie hear my response and laugh even though it wasn't my intention to be funny. "I'm feeling a little light-headed. Can I go sit in the cabin for a bit?" I ask.

"Of course. You know you could be getting seasick," says Davie. "Arturo got seasick the first time I brought him out."

"Do you want me to go with you?" asks Chris.

"No, I'm feeling a bit agitated. I need some time to get my bearings if that's okay."

The three men say in unison, "Yes, go ahead."

When I get to the cabin, I shut the door.

CHAPTER 33

The Journey Begins

Light is sparse in the cabin with the door closed. I notice the windows are tinted as I lie on a short bench. The thought of the bee from earlier causes me to jump up in a panic. The fluttering, stinging insect could still be in this cabin. I see the jar on the ground secured into place by a table leg. I sit up suddenly and go to open the cabin door all the way. As the light penetrates the room, I can see dust particles dance through the beams of light. Most of the particles settle toward the ground, except for about an eighth of them, which gravitate up toward the sunlight. I grab the jar and turn it over on the small table. There is some moisture in the glass. I can see subtle streaks of bait residue glisten on the inside of the jar. As I peer closely at it, I think about the bee again. It weakly fluttered around at the bottom of the jar—it must have been sick. When I opened the jar slightly, however, it tried to escape full force with lightning speed. It could have gotten away too if it would have stopped jumping and concentrated on getting out through the open air pocket. After I had put the envelope underneath the jar as a seal, it sat there in despair.

I reanalyze what it must be like to be the bee. I'm like the bee caught inside the jar, except that I am on the outside without wings. The wings are locked inside the jar, and I fight to break into the glass prison because I can't go anywhere without my wings. I don't know how much of a problem getting out of the jar would be if I were successful in getting my wings, but I'll worry about that if or when I can get to them.

A knock on the door breaks my dreamy state of consciousness. Arturo enters and asks in his most avuncular tone, "How you feeling, kiddo?"

"I don't feel well. Just let me stay down here for a while, and I'll be fine," I say.

"You look pale. Try not to throw up in the cabin; Davie will roast me."

"I'm okay. Just need a little time to be by myself."

He gets the hint and tells me to let him know if I need anything before he leaves, closing the door.

Once he's gone, I start to acquire a fever. My forehead is hot to the touch, and my ears feel hot too. I start to become catatonic. It's hard for me to move about the slightest bit. I need to break free from this catatonic state, but how? I start to take shallow breaths and can no longer breathe in an involuntary way. I have to consciously make myself suck air into my lungs as well as push it out. If I don't, I believe that I will stop breathing. I think that maybe it won't be so bad, so I stop consciously breathing. After about ten seconds, I am now suffocating. I look down at the ground to see if it's clean enough for me to fall unconscious onto it when I see what looks like a little dark piece of chocolate moving my way. I must be hallucinating. I strain my eyes to see the object better in the dark cabin and notice that it is some kind of insect making its way toward me. It slowly comes closer, and I finally recognize it: it is a bee—the bee perhaps that I encountered earlier. It is solidly dark without any of its yellow colors showing since the room is dimly lit. I consciously take in a deep breath. I cannot take the straining pain anymore from not breathing. When I consciously exhale, my breath comes out in ripples. The bee starts to fly toward me, makes a sharp 180-degree turn, and flies to the tinted glass pane on the door. It buzzes near it before it completely stops moving and sits on the little seal where the window meets the door. I quickly jump out of my catatonic state and run to the door and open it, and out flies the bee. Will it survive? Yes, for now, but it's got a lot of uncharted territory to cover since it's been taken out to sea many miles away from land. Can it make the journey across the ocean? I don't know. I don't know what bees can do.

Printed in the United States
By Bookmasters